# SIR ANDREW AND THE AUTHORESS

# SIR
# ANDREW
## *and the*
# AUTHORESS

CLAIRVOIR CASTLE *Romances*
BOOK THREE

# SALLY BRITTON

Sally Britton
www.authorsallybritton.com

First Printing: April 2022

*To my Sally Squad: Thank you for your enthusiasm and your encouragement!*

# CHAPTER 1
## LONDON, ENGLAND

March 22nd, 1819

"The worst thing about London in the Spring," Sir Andrew said with a disapproving frown, "is the myriad of people who come out of doors to crowd the parks." Indeed, carriages and horses packed Rotten Row tightly enough that riding at anything faster than a tortoise's pace proved impossible.

The baronet's best friend merely chuckled, too used to Andrew's horse-madness to take the complaint seriously. Simon Dinard, called by his honorary title of Lord Farleigh, wore confidence the way others slipped on a pair of old gloves. With comfort and the ease of habit.

"We are here until June, at least," Simon reminded him. "Though my father believes the current unrest might keep him through most of the summer." The duke's heir nodded to an acquaintance in passing but did not stop. They were late.

Sometimes, Andrew envied his friend's self-possession. Simon came by it naturally, as the eldest son and heir of the Duke of Montfort. Andrew emphatically did *not* envy Simon's title or future responsibilities in the least. The heir to the duchy carried more responsibility on his shoulders than most men in England.

Simon led them out of the park when they finally came to the end of the Row, ostensibly ignoring a barouche filled with young ladies all batting their eyelashes at him. Yet another thing Andrew had no wish to possess—an army of female admirers. The marriageable daughters of England's nobility would throw themselves in front of Simon's charging horse if they thought it meant a chance to gain his attention.

"While I appreciate the Duke's invitation to these meetings, I still wonder at my inclusion." Andrew turned enough in his saddle to see Simon's bodyguard following on his own mount at a short distance. "I have no wish to pursue a career in politics." He couldn't imagine dedicating his life to arguing with a room full of men more stubborn than him. He'd much rather enjoy life than waste time trying to shout down anyone who didn't share his perspective.

"You say that now." Simon wove between two carriages, with Andrew following close behind. "But if you ever change your mind, these afternoons with my father will prove useful."

The Duke of Montfort had always allowed Andrew a place in his home. Years ago, His Grace had been friends with Andrew's father. When an illness left Andrew a baronet at only nineteen years old, His Grace brought Andrew fully into the family. Andrew even had his own set of rooms in each of the Montfort family's residences.

Everyone had made him feel welcome. Except for Josephine. The Duke's eldest daughter. Though she was five years his junior, she had treated him with indifference for several years, and then annoyance. Which he found entertaining enough to needle her into that state all the more, and he grinned to himself at the thought of seeing her. Needling her just enough to see the blush rise in her cheeks and her eyes grow stormy as she calculated the best response to put him in his place.

As Andrew and Simon maneuvered through the crowded streets, clouds gathered above to turn the cheerful day into something somber. By the time they reached the duke's London house, the bright blue sky had transitioned into a mournful shade of gray.

They entered the house at the same time a distant roll of thunder echoed across the rooftops of London. Josephine Dinard, eldest daughter of the duke and duchess, stood on the stairs that descended into the entryway. She wore clothing meant for a walk, including gloves and bonnet.

"Was that thunder?" she asked, taking the last several steps in a rush, her long pelisse flying up behind her like a cape. "Do not say it was thunder!"

"Very well." Andrew spoke before Simon could say a word. "I will not say so. What shall it be instead? A giant's game of nine pins? Perhaps the inexcusable rumblings of a hungry tiger?"

Josephine cast him a look of disdain before going to the large window nearest the door and peering out. "Mother and I were to go out."

Simon and Andrew shared a glance—Andrew of some amusement, which faded when he realized his friend appeared concerned.

"You might still go to the Arcade," Simon said somewhat consolingly. The Burlington Arcade, a covered shopping avenue newly constructed by George Cavendish, Earl of Burlington, featured nearly seventy shops full of luxury goods. The Arcade had opened only the week before. The family had missed the grand opening because of a wedding in the country.

His sister slowly shook her head. "No. You know how little mother enjoys shopping." She turned from the window, the disappointment darkening her blue eyes.

She went to the stairs without another word, as gloomy as the weather outside. She didn't even bother to glare at Andrew, and he couldn't find it in himself to tease her.

Andrew looked at Simon again, puzzled, but his friend gestured to the hall. His father's study was in another wing of the house, which meant they could ascend to the correct level at a different flight of stairs. Andrew followed, and after they turned a corner, Simon finally explained.

"You left directly after the wedding," he said. "But ever since Josie waved farewell to Emma's carriage, she's been a bit out of sorts."

Emma Arlen, now the Contessa di Atella, had been Josephine's companion. And her best friend since their nursery years. She also happened to be Andrew's first-cousin, on his mother's side. Emma had fallen in love with one of the duke's summer guests—an ambassador from the Kingdom of the Two Sicilies. They had married only a fortnight ago.

"Have they never been apart?" Andrew asked, frowning. "I know Emma visited our relatives from time to time."

"Yes, but she always planned to return." Simon led them up a staircase, his expression still dark. "This time, Emma isn't coming back. Not for more than a visit. They were close as sisters."

Simon and Josephine had other siblings, of course. Two younger sisters and a brother. But there were several years between Josephine and her next sister. Too many years for them to go about in Society together.

"Will she find another paid companion?" Andrew asked. "She must be lonely. I cannot think she has ever been without Emma for more than a few days."

"No one has dared to bring it up yet. We all know she will deny she needs a companion. Whenever anyone mentions Emma, Josephine only says how happy she is for the marriage." Simon led them through a set of doors through the library, a long room decorated in rich greens and expansive maps, with quite possibly the most comfortable furniture in the whole house pulled up to three different fireplaces. They stopped at the next set of doors. Simon tapped on one of the large wooden panels.

The duke answered from within his study. "Enter."

Simon opened the door and entered first with Andrew directly behind him. In appearance, the study was an extension of the library. Deep green wallpaper covered the walls not hidden by tall bookcases, and thick rugs with patterns of twisting vines and flowers covered the dark-planked floors. Along two walls were tall windows. One set of windows looked into the courtyard, the other looked over the street below.

Gregory Dinard, the fifth Duke of Montfort, stood with his back to them. His hands were clasped behind him, and he stared out the window to the carriages and people below. "Simon. Andrew." The brief greeting had both younger men instantly pausing in their steps.

The duke never addressed them by their Christian names except when they were together as a family. In his political meetings with them, he used their titles. While the difference might be subtle to some, it immediately indicated the nature of their conversation was not what they had expected.

"Father." Simon waited until the duke turned around, and Andrew watched as the man he admired above all others slowly faced them. His shoulders rounded, as though bearing a weight, and his eyes looked from one man to the other with solemnity.

"Please, sit. There is something we need to discuss."

They sat in the chairs across from the duke's desk. Rather than retake his own seat, the duke went to his desk only to take a paper from its drawers. He came around to their side and held it out to Simon. "Read this."

Andrew waited as Simon read in silence, then took the paper and read it for himself. The letter, signed by none other than the Earl of Liverpool, who currently served as Prime Minister, informed the duke of acts of sedition and rebellion across England. It strongly urged the duke to reconsider his stance on renewing the bill to prevent public gatherings—something the duke had disagreed with when a temporary law was put in place two years before.

But what His Grace likely wanted to discuss was near the end of the letter. Along with the information and plea, the prime minister warned that several members of Parliament had been attacked on the street. What started as members of the public shouting slurs outside of Parliament itself, according to the letter, had escalated to stones hurled at carriage windows.

Andrew read the last line of warning aloud. "'It is no secret that the Duke of Montfort is a powerful voice in the government. Guard yourself and your family as best you can.'"

"I cannot think we have much to concern ourselves over," Simon said when Andrew lowered the letter. "Rockwell follows me everywhere. Mother has two of your men with her whenever she leaves the house, the governess and children never leave unescorted. Josephine, too."

Andrew nodded in agreement without thinking. When Andrew joined the family after his father's death, the duke had informed him of the measures he took to secure their safety. Former soldiers stood as guards throughout the house, though they dressed and acted as footmen. His carriage drivers were always armed. Every private room in the house had expensive locks installed. There were hidden passageways for family to step into and disappear entirely from sight if necessary. Even Simon rarely went anywhere unarmed—his walking stick concealed a blade he wielded with expertise.

"I have always guarded against the possibility of a threat," the duke said, accepting the letter from Andrew. "We have had little to trouble us due to my precautions. But this is different. Our countrymen are spoiling for a fight. And I cannot say I blame them," he added, voice low.

Their previous conversations in this room had given Andrew enough knowledge to understand the duke's frustration. Corn laws, new taxes and tariffs, Luddites, rotten boroughs, and a people wanting more from their government than the government was willing to give, had brought them to the edge of a precipice.

Would the government topple? Would the people? Or would everyone slowly back away and return to a discontented quiet?

They had France to look to for an example of what *could* happen. Revolution. Treason. Death. Battle in the high streets of their cities. The government couldn't ignore the rising voices of its citizens. Yet no one offered solutions except to press the people back into submission.

"I must ask you both for greater vigilance," the duke said into the thick quiet, his words pressing into Andrew's grim thoughts. "When you are out, look after each other. When you can, look after the others in this household. Andrew, anyone with a knowledge of my family knows I consider you as a son. I fear you might be in some danger because of that."

Andrew's heart swelled with pride, and his head spun with the impact of the duke's words. Though he had always felt part of the family, on an intimate level with them that was difficult to explain, it had never been stated so boldly by the duke before. "The affection you and your family have shown me are worth any danger, Your Grace."

The duke's smile appeared, though tempered still by the atmosphere. "We have months left in London yet. I fear as the weather grows warm, so too will tempers rise. Be wary. Stay alert when you are not within the safety of this house."

"Yes, Father."

"Yes, Your Grace."

"I will speak with the duchess to determine how much of the circumstances we will share with the children. I have no wish to frighten those under my care, but I cannot think it wise to leave them without any word of this." The duke walked around to the other side of the desk and took his seat. "Now then. We have a circumstance in Parliament regarding the right to trial by combat —an ancient law yet to be repealed."

The subject changed. The three men began a different conversation altogether. Andrew took the duke's warnings to heart, of course. Right along with the knowledge that His Grace, the Duke of Montfort, thought of him as a son.

# CHAPTER 2

R ain pattered against the cobblestones outside for the third
day in a row. Josie watched as the droplets ran down the
window pane, joining one another to create long trails of water as
they raced across the glass. She sat at her writing desk, leaning
against the back of her chair, her pen forgotten atop the letter on
the desk's surface.

Lady Josephine had written three letters of regret that day. As
though anyone would question whether she would come for their
picnics and park walks, given the constant weeping of the sky.

She rubbed at her eyes and left her chair, knowing the last
letter she needed to write would keep until later. She had to move.
Sitting still for hours at a time did not agree with her. Not here in
London. Not when every moment of being still reminded her of
her failure.

Without meaning to, Josie glanced at the top of her wardrobe.
There, concealed by the furniture's ornately carved peacock, was
a box filled with paper. A whole stack of expensive, beautiful
paper onto which she had poured out her imagination and all the
lovely words she knew. And at the top of the stack, much smaller

and cheaply made, was a letter from a publisher. Rejecting the work of her *nom de plume* as "unpublishable."

She turned away, her cheeks burning anew with shame, and left her room.

Immature.

Inexperienced.

And worst of all, *ignorant.*

All words in that rejection letter. All directed at her and her manuscript. A story she had conceived and believed in the moment the idea had crossed her mind to become an author. She, a woman better educated than almost any other, had failed to write a work of fiction well enough for a publisher to even entertain the idea of printing it.

Josie went down the long corridor of the family's rooms without paying much attention to her surroundings. She knew every corner and crevice of her father's London home. Half her life she'd roamed the halls, played in the attic, and hidden behind curtains in this house. It was nearly as beloved to her as Castle Clairvoir.

Where she would much rather be, away from all her duties, lest someone notice her morose turn of mind.

The rejection humiliated her. And there was no one with whom she could share her distress. Her one and only confidant, Emma, had married and was in the midst of her honeymoon. She would not return to the embassy, where she would live with her ambassador husband during his service to his country, for another week.

At least no one knew.

If Josie could only distract herself, she might even forget for a time that her dream of writing had died an unfortunate death with less than one-hundred words from a publisher. It was a small grace that the man had been blessedly brief in his rejection. Josie knew ladies who had taken many times that number of words to decline their suitors.

Josie drifted through the music room, then the open doorway leading to the parlor that overlooked the street. On the opposite wing of the house, her father's study had a similar view. She watched as a couple with one umbrella between them walked slowly through the rain. She couldn't see their faces, but the man had tucked the woman close to his side to keep her warm and dry.

Carriages rolled by, the horses dripping with water, the coachmen appearing cross beneath their hats and oil-slicked coats.

The parlor door opened. "Here you are, Josephine." Cecilia, the Duchess of Montfort, had found her.

Josie turned, hiding her thoughts behind a smile. "Mama. Were you looking for me?"

When Josie looked at her mother, she often make-believed she was looking at herself in the future. Mother and daughter held many similarities in face and form. The duchess's figure had filled out with her years of bearing children, yet she maintained a lightness of step that made it appear as though she floated across the ground. She wore her dark hair styled to look like the ancient women of Greece.

"I was about to send for you." Her mother came into the room, pulling her shawl closer about her shoulders. She moved with a grace that Josie had tried to emulate all her life. "Have you sent our regrets yet?"

"All but one," Josie answered. "The Rollins' garden party is this evening. I will be certain our note gets to them soon."

"Thank you. No one will expect us, I am certain." The duchess lowered herself regally into a chair near the fire. "This has been a rather disappointing week for you, I am afraid."

"It's quite all right." Josie took the chair facing her mother across the cream-colored carpet. "I thought we might go to the theater this evening since that is one place we might not get wet."

Her mother considered for a moment. "I am not certain how comfortable your father will be with that idea. We would need to take two or three men with us, and where would they be the whole of the play? They can hardly stand in our box with us, but otherwise they would crowd the hall."

Josie winced. Her father's new precautions for the family's safety had momentarily slipped her mind. "We cannot go anywhere?" she asked softly. "What of the museums? We could go see the Egyptian exhibit, or the Marbles."

"Perhaps." The duchess regarded Josie with a thoughtful tilt of her head. "Have you had any word from Emma?"

"Of course not." Josie tried and failed to hide her amusement. "Emma is two weeks married. If she wrote me a letter while on her honeymoon, it would astound me. She is far too in love to pay any heed to anyone or anything other than her count."

"I am glad you are happy for her."

"How could I be anything other than happy?" Josie directed her gaze away from her mother, looking down at her fingers as she fiddled with a ring on her index finger. "She fell in love, even though she once told me she did not think it would ever happen to her."

"I suppose you are the more romantically inclined," her mother murmured. When Josie looked up, she saw her mother's wistful smile. "You are nearly twenty years old, Josie."

"In three weeks." Josie wrinkled her nose. "Should I ask for a pony for my birthday?"

The duchess laughed, as though genuinely surprised by her daughter. "No, you naughty girl. Your father might not understand the joke and procure you another mean-spirited little thing."

"Buttercup wasn't all that terrible, was he?" she asked, referring to the pony she'd received on her eighth birthday. "Though I do remember him throwing me off his back on occasion."

"And he tried to bite anyone who came within six feet of him," her mother added, shaking her head merrily. "He had the very worst disposition. No more ponies for you, my dear."

"What ought a twenty-year-old lady ask for, then? Hm?" Josie wiggled her toes. "New slippers?"

"Perhaps if you were not a duke's daughter."

"Oh, you wish me to think more extravagantly. An entirely new gown, then? Embroidered with pearls."

"Or jewels," her mother put in, joining in the game. "Diamonds or rubies."

"Perhaps a tiara. Or a carriage of my own and a team of matching horses."

The duchess leaned back into her chair, smiling. "Now we are getting somewhere. A carriage. Emma always wanted to travel. Do you?"

"Not particularly. Our visit to France after the war was more than enough for me." She hadn't done particularly well on the sea crossing, despite the calm waters. "Though I suppose I will visit Emma at her husband's home someday."

"Not travel." Her mother raised a hand to her cheek and pursed her lips. "What is it you want to do with yourself?" The question dropped softly between them, featherlight and unworried.

They had talked of this before over the years, but Josie sensed a difference in the question this time. Whether it was in how her mother asked or within Josie herself, she couldn't be certain.

She looked down at her hands again. Her mother couldn't know what Josie wanted most of all—to write novels. To have them published. As a duke's daughter, she would bring gossip and censure upon the whole family if she did such a thing. Especially if critics disliked her work.

Finally, she answered with a weak shake of her head. "I want nothing, Mama. I have everything I could ever ask for." She twisted the ring around her finger once, then forced herself to laugh. "I suppose things will continue on as they have. I will keep learning from you and from Grandmama, and I will help to keep up the house and social obligations."

The duchess released a short, brisk breath. "How dreadfully dull that sounds."

Josephine blinked at her mother. "Would you rather I take up mountain-climbing?"

"Of course not. I would rather you enjoy yourself more."

"Mama. We both know that when *you* were my age, your idea of enjoyment was visiting houses and buildings under construction so you could sketch them."

"True." When her mother smiled, Josie couldn't resist grinning back at her. "I also attended my share of parties, balls, and everything else."

"I do those things. I am hardly a hermit." Josie stood and moved to the fireplace, pretending to study one of the small Parisian figurines upon it. Her parents had bought the replica of a seventeenth century musketeer, along with his lady, and both now stood on either side of the mantel clock. Forever separated by *time*, of all things.

"Yes, but I have yet to see you take a personal interest in anything." Her mother rose and joined her, studying first Josie's face and then the little musketeer. "Or in any man."

Josie started. "A man? Mama, I am only nineteen."

The duchess raised one hand to stay her daughter's protests. "I know, my dear. Nearly twenty. Your father and I have no expectations for you to marry merely because you reach a certain age, whether it is twenty or seventy."

Having heard this well-meant lecture many times in her life, Josie recited the rest of it by rote. "So long as your children are happy, you are content. And you wish us to marry where we have genuine affection, rather than as a matter of convenience. Yes, I know."

The duchess lifted her head, her bearing regal once more. "Good. Never forget it." Then she gave Josie an affectionate kiss upon the cheek. Josie closed her eyes and inhaled the sweet scent of her mother's lavender perfume. "I must look in on your grandmother. She hasn't left her rooms today."

Josie looked to the clock. It was nearly two in the afternoon. "It is late. Even if the dreary weather puts her out of sorts, she is usually about by now. I will come with you."

"An excellent idea. Come. We will ply her with tea and sweets until she is happy again, and then you may ask her what she received as a gift for her twentieth birthday." The way the duchess's eyes sparkled meant mischief, and Josie happily gave herself over to the idea.

Josie looked again at the musketeer and his lady on the other side of the mantel. Pursing her lips, she lifted the musketeer and placed him beside his lady, pushing the mantel clock over enough to make room. She grinned to herself, then she followed her mother from the room.

She would happily offer distraction to her grandmother, and do anything else that would take her mind off her manuscript and her father's additional security measures.

# CHAPTER 3

Although acquainted with many, Josephine had few genuine friends. Her companion, Emma, had been the person closest to her for most of her life. Until Emma returned from her tour of Scotland and Wales with her new husband, Josephine had to find other young ladies to accompany her on visits and shopping trips.

Which meant inviting some of those acquaintances to visit her home, so they might walk to the Burlington Arcade to visit the shops. Somewhat predictably, her guests looked over their shoulders quite often at Josie's accompanying footman.

"My father would never let an upper-servant follow me about all day," Lady Helen said, using the reflection in a shop's glass to peer behind her at the vigilant man.

"Especially one so attractive." Miss Lesley's smirk was full of more mischief than *her* father would likely approve of.

Lady Helen giggled behind her hand. "How does one find such servants, Lady Josephine? All of ours are either gray-haired ancients or speckled juveniles."

They did not know that the footman, tall, handsome, and an upper servant in the duke's household, was also a guardsman. His duty had little to do with carrying the occasional parcel and much more with the various weapons hidden about his person.

"Sterling has his uses," Josie said airily. "Oh, look at that darling pair of earrings." Distracting them from her guard was easy enough. The women gathered around a shop window to coo over baubles most of them could not afford with their pin money, despite being the daughters of the wealthiest men in the kingdom.

Josie looked over her shoulder at her guard, who made only brief eye contact with her before his eyes slid away to study the others in the long corridor of shops. Sterling was a newer member of the household staff, but thus far, he'd proved himself an alert and responsible guard.

They stopped at a milliner's window next. "I cannot understand the fashion of wearing dead birds atop one's bonnet." Lady Helen scrutinized a large bonnet complete with bird's nest and stuffed dove.

Miss Lesley wrinkled her nose. "It sounds terribly morbid when you describe it that way. Do you know what I wonder? Why the women of England are well-feathered and the men always dress so dull, in their blues and blacks. Did you know that in the French court the men dressed as finely, if not more so, than the women? And that was only a generation or two ago."

"I have no desire to be escorted anywhere by a man better dressed than I am," Lady Helen said. "What about you, Lady Josephine?"

Josie didn't particularly care for the topic, so she only shrugged. "I suppose not."

"Your brother always looks well groomed and tailored," Lady Helen said, her eyes narrowing to speculative slits. "And that friend of his he always goes about with."

"Sir Andrew," Josie supplied. "I cannot say either of them have set about to be fashionable. I cannot recall ever hearing them speak about such things."

"Is Sir Andrew often with your family?" Miss Lesley asked. "He certainly is handsome."

"Troublesome, I should think," Josie muttered.

Lady Helen didn't seem to have heard her, as she took up the topic with zeal. "Oh, he is a delightful man. A marvelous dancer, and I have heard he is quite witty. But I cannot say I have ever been so fortunate as to have seen that wit."

"Truly?" Josie turned away from the window she had peered through a moment before. "I would think he'd flirted with half the women in London by now."

Miss Lesley and Lady Helen exchanged a wide-eyed glance. "I have never heard he has a reputation of that sort." Miss Lesley adjusted the strings of the reticule at her wrist. "But now I think I ought to take it as an insult that he hasn't flirted with me before. What a shame. He is—"

"Handsome, yes. So you said." Lady Helen scoffed. "Oh, what are those charming little dolls in that window?" She leaned closer to scrutinize the delicate toys. "I have a niece who would adore that one, with the lace veil."

Though the excuse of shopping with friends allowed Josephine to leave the house, the less than challenging conversation did not distract her enough. Although it did surprise her, somewhat, to know Andrew wasn't considered a flirt.

As she had no wish to think on Andrew at present, she continued to turn over in her mind the plot of her novel. Had she made her hero too weak? Her heroine too strong? If only that horrid rejection letter had contained more specifics. The manuscript as a whole could not be so terrible, could it?

Josephine had considered herself mature beyond her years. The daughter of a duke ought to be more worldly than the daughter of a country clergyman. As that was precisely the situation of her heroine, she had truly thought herself equal to the task of writing about such a woman.

She wandered to the next shop ahead of her friends, looking

through the glass to a perfumery. The shopkeeper had arranged dozens of bottles upon shelves, all of them different hues and shapes, and decorated the window's corners with sprays of flowers to illustrate the scents that might be found within.

She stared through the glass, lips pursed, not truly focusing on the wares in front of her.

"Contemplating the serious nature of your personal odor, Josie?"

Her gaze flicked up to see the reflection of a certain fair-haired, dark-eyed irritant grinning at her. She narrowed her eyes at Sir Andrew. "I thought to make a present to you, but then I realized if I masked your current scent too well, I would not know of your approach in time to prepare myself for your company."

"You recognize me by scent?" His eyes danced and his grin widened. "I hadn't any inkling you paid attention to such personal details. Ought I to be flattered?"

She turned to look at him instead of the reflected image and batted her eyes as she said, "Only as flattered as a dog when scented by a doe."

His eyes narrowed. "You view me as a hunter, my lady? With you as my quarry?"

"Not at all. I view you as an unpleasant disturbance to my day. A disturbance that smells strongly of dog."

His grin returned, sharper than before. "Thus the contemplation of perfumes." He nodded to the shop window. "But you know you cannot appreciate them from out here."

"I have no intention of entering the shop today. I am merely admiring the window dressings with my friends."

"Friends?" He arched his eyebrows at her. "What friends?"

She parted her lips to name them, turning as she did to where she had left the two ladies, but she found the spot they had occupied taken up by an older woman and her maid. Josie frowned and turned around, her eyes sweeping the Arcade and finding both Lady Helen and Miss Lesley nowhere in sight. She looked to her guard, who stood on the opposite side of the arcade, watching the area with care.

"They must have gone into one of the shops," she said at last. "I am certain they will return momentarily." Her thoughts had not made her inattentive overlong.

"As you say." Andrew looked down the long, covered pathway to the end opposite where she and her friends had entered. The Burlington Arcade stretched from Piccadilly to Burlington Gardens. At nearly two-hundred yards in length, it had been quite an ambitious undertaking by the Earl of Burlington. Andrew, however, seemed unimpressed.

Josie walked in an unhurried manner to the next storefront—a window full of books. She scowled at the bound covers and went on again, irritably aware that Andrew followed behind. She stopped in front of the next window to find it full of fine paper and cleverly displayed dipping pens. Small signs shared what they made the paper of, whether it had a linen finish or something the seller called a 'cotton soft sheet.'

The pens were what fascinated her. The duke had the best quills in every desk of his houses. They were from peacocks and swans, and double-quilled. But the idea of a pen which one could use over and over instead of continually reshaping and eventually discarding—it appealed to her.

"What has your attention now?" Andrew asked from over her shoulder, standing nearer than strictly necessary. He likely attempted to annoy her.

"Pens," she said. "Have you used one? Father has always insisted on quills."

Andrew leaned closer to the glass and nearer her shoulder. When he spoke, his breath tickled the bare skin of her neck. "It seems more economical to use something like this. Which isn't something a duke need worry about, is it?"

She stiffened. "My father is hardly a spendthrift." She had to turn nearly all the way to see him around the edges of her bonnet, but it was worth it to better look daggers at him.

He rocked back on his heels, moving away to a more respectable distance. "I would never say such a thing of him, either. I mean to say that your father has no need to change habits. If a quill suits him, because he can afford the finest available, why rely upon metal-tipped rods of wood?"

"Hm." She cast one more look at the pens, then tried to find her companions in the milling crowd again. They were nowhere in sight. Where had they gone off to? And why had they not thought to bring her with them? Though conditioned to ignore Sterling, as someone of her standing must ignore a servant, she prepared to summon him to ask after her friends—but her guard glared fixedly down the Arcade's length.

That was when she heard the shouts.

"Gormless nobs," someone yelled, voice echoing through the covered lane. "Buyin' up your fancies and baubles while men starve on the street!"

Most of the people in the arcade were women from fine houses. Like Josephine. There were gasps and cries of outrage, but no one moved toward the person shouting. Instead, the shouts grew louder as three men stormed down the pathway, dressed in clothing marking them as part of the working class.

One of them spit near the feet of a finely dressed woman, who withdrew to press against a shop window. Other women were darting into the shops, faces pale.

Sterling had crossed to Josephine, standing between her and the approaching men.

"Get her inside," Sir Andrew growled to Sterling, watching the oncoming men with a fierce glare. Then he stepped directly into the path of the oncoming men. They were only a third of the way through the arcade where Josephine stood.

Sterling nodded to the shop behind her. "If you would, my lady."

If she didn't do as the guard said, her father would hear of it, and she would be the one facing a displeased duke. Josephine slipped backward to the shop door and ducked inside. Her guard remained at the door, on the outside.

The man behind the countertop immediately greeted her with cheer. Josie smiled tightly at him and went to the window to peer out. Andrew wouldn't really confront anyone, would he? The men would pass by, venting their displeasure, and that would be an end to it.

But as she looked between the display shelves of paper and metal-tipped pens, she saw the baronet standing in the center of the arcade, legs apart, chin up, and posture rather like a tiger waiting to spring. She could not make out his words, muffled as they were by the glass and the sounds outside.

"May I help you find something in particular, miss...?" the pen merchant asked from behind her.

Josie waved in his direction, not taking her eyes from the three men Andrew addressed. "Yes, in one moment. I am looking at this display."

Her single comment induced him to a great deal more chatter. "Oh, yes. The new pens. They are a marvel. A perfect gift, too, for any gentlemen in your life. A father, perhaps, or a brother. I have others with fine carving in the wood, dyed to any color you wish."

Outside the shop, the three men all glared at Andrew, flexing their hands and appearing ready to charge him. But then Andrew barked, the single word at a volume loud enough even for her to hear clearly. "Enough!" He gestured back the way they had come. The men startled, as did Josephine.

THOUGH TEACHING THE THREE RUFFIANS IN FRONT OF HIM A lesson through fisticuffs would prove satisfying, it certainly would not be appropriate. Especially given the number of females already watching the verbal altercation.

"Enough," Andrew shouted when one of them dared drop a slur against the innocent women shopping that day. "By now, someone has called a constable to deal with your petulant whining. Your display before these women, wives and daughters as gentle as your own, is at an end. Only cowards would assault those who dare not oppose them, speaking filth and acting lower than dogs. Leave now, peacefully, or I will take it upon myself to throw you into the street as you deserve."

The man standing in the middle, broader than the other two but still a head shorter than Andrew, sized him up with slitted eyes and his chin thrust forward like a weapon. His gaze flicked from Andrew to the Arcade's patrons on one side and Sterling on the other.

He spat on the ground again, then jerked his head back. "You wait, Lord Muck. The people won't let your kind rule us forever." He backed up a step, the men on either side of him doing the same, then they turned and went back the way they came. One of them whistled as he went, and another laughed raucously until they passed out onto the street.

What were rough men like that doing, walking down Piccadilly in *this* neighborhood at this time of day? How did they even dare cross beneath the ceiling of the Arcade? Burlington had built the thoroughfare—some said—specifically so the women of his acquaintance might enjoy high-end shops without having to travel to the less-savory streets of London.

"Burlington ought to employ guards," Andrew muttered, then turned his attention to Sterling, Josephine's guard for the day. He held open the door to the shop, and his charge came out with wide eyes and a quick glance in the direction the men had exited.

"What was all that about?" she asked, her voice soft and manner more hesitant than usual.

Andrew studied her face a moment, ensuring she hadn't been

overly frightened. Josephine appeared perfectly calm. She hadn't even turned pale. He looked the same direction as she. "Cowardly men, making a scene. Harassing those who represent all that they despise, though they have nothing to do with it."

Women all along the Arcade were speaking in whispers to each other, and there were a few nervous titters, too. A door several shops down opened, and two ladies came out, a maid with them, and hurried to Josephine. They both started talking to her at once, which gave Andrew leave to surmise they were the friends who had earlier abandoned her.

The duke's daughter spoke over them in an obvious attempt to gain their attention. "Yes, I know. It was dreadful. Since we cannot be sure if those men, or more like them, will come back, let us return to my house. We can have refreshment there, and my father's carriage will return you both home."

That met with the other ladies' approval, and Andrew didn't think he'd imagined the way Sterling relaxed at the shoulders, either. The guard would want his charge safely at home so he could make his report.

Josephine sent him one last glance, concern in her eyes. Andrew grinned at her, as though nothing had happened, eliciting a small frown from the duke's daughter. Then she let her friends tug her toward Piccadilly Street where it was a short walk back to her father's doors.

Andrew watched her go, fully intending to follow. First, he ducked into the shop where Josephine had taken refuge. The shopkeeper inside, an older gentleman with spectacles at the tip of his nose and carefully combed graying hair, brightened when he met Andrew's gaze.

"Good day to you, sir. Have you a need for pens, pencils, charcoal, stationary, or paper today?"

"Pens, actually." Andrew went to the display where Josephine had peered with interest before the little drama had occurred. He found a case containing three pens, the wooden bodies expertly carved with ivy and the metal nibs shining on the end, bright and new. He picked up the case and brought it to the proprietor. "I think these will do. What of ink?"

"Yes, of course. I have the finest ink available. Do you need something other than black?"

He thought of Josephine's startled, wide blue eyes and smiled to himself. "Indigo. If you have it."

For as long as he'd known Josephine, she'd always scribbled away at letters, poetry she refused to let him or anyone else read, and who knew what else. That she had marveled over so simple an instrument as a pen had amused him, of course. Why not gift her the thing he doubted she would buy for herself?

Despite all their teasing, their playful bickering, he counted her a friend. And she did have a birthday approaching. Why not offer an olive branch, of sorts?

After making his purchase and directing the delivery to his rented rooms, Andrew went to the duke's house. The duke himself would be in Parliament, but Simon was likely home. Andrew had been on his way to meet his friend when he'd caught sight of Josephine entering the Arcade. He'd changed his path without thinking. Now he was glad he had.

Sterling could easily have dispatched the three hostile men had there been a threat to Josephine, but he would do nothing if his charge wasn't under direct threat. Doing so would further compromise Josephine's safety, and his mission given him by the duke was singular in purpose. That left all those other women exposed to vulgarity and verbal abuse. Something Andrew would not stand for.

The duke's admonition for the family to take greater care had proved prophetic. If the political agitators had emboldened their followers to harass the upper classes and nobility with such boldness, things might get much worse before the end of the Parliamentary session.

He entered Dinard House as normal, handing off hat and

gloves to the footman who greeted him. The staff treated him as one of the family, allowing him to come and go as he wished with little fuss. The servant informed him that Simon had last been in his mother's favorite sitting room.

As Andrew approached the door, he heard several voices within. He adjusted the lapels of his coat and nodded to the manservant stationed outside the door to open it for him. Then he walked inside, hearing the duchess's words first.

"Calm yourselves, my dear young ladies. You are all quite safe now, and indeed, I do not think you were in real danger of more than hearing unpleasant men speak unpleasant words." The duchess sat on a plumply cushioned chair with Josephine on a matching footstool before her. The other two young women who had been with Josephine before were on a couch, still wearing bonnets, though both had teacups in ungloved hands. The dowager duchess sat in a chair opposite the rug from her daughter-in-law, and the two younger daughters of the duke were on a loveseat, their eyes wide and hands gripping their embroidery hoops.

Simon stood as far away from the knot of females as he could, his back to a window, and glared fiercely at the fireplace. If Andrew had his way, he'd have slunk quietly and unnoticed around the edge of the room until he reached Simon—or else the two of them would have escaped altogether.

Instead, the dowager duchess saw him and addressed him with all her usual pomp and solemnity.

"Sir Andrew. I have not seen you in an age, young man." She held her hand toward him, and he had to bite back a chuckle as he approached her. Most of the family saw the dowager as a formidable, though loving, individual. He had even heard his cousin Emma refer to her as an old dragon. Somehow, he'd always been a favorite of hers.

"Your Grace." He took her hand and bowed over it. "I am flattered you noticed my absence."

SALLY BRITTON

"As well you should be." The woman's eyes twinkled up at him. "Up to some mischief, no doubt. Have you met Josephine's friends?"

Andrew turned and bowed to the young ladies now standing for their introduction. Lady Josephine reluctantly stood and set matters to right. Once everyone was acquainted, she retook her seat at her mother's feet.

The duchess waited long enough for Andrew to join her son at the window before she said, "Sir Andrew, Josephine was just telling us of the unfortunate encounter at the Arcade today."

"Yes. It was unpleasant." He smiled as he used her own word, then added, "But nothing to concern yourself over, Your Grace. The men went on their way. Though I do think His Grace might speak to Lord Burlington about hiring guards or employing beadles to patrol the area. For safety's sake."

"Do you think it will happen again?" Lady Helen asked, her voice pitched higher than Andrew found comfortable. "Papa will never let me go to the Arcade again if he hears of this."

Andrew tried not to wince as he answered her. "I doubt we will have another incident. But as the lane is narrow and full of gentlewomen and their purchases, it makes sense to have someone there to watch over their security."

Simon spoke, his tone dark. "We can hope for continued safety, but I imagine many fathers will take steps to protect their daughters, Lady Helen."

She simpered up at Simon, as most unattached females did. "I suppose it is given to women to submit to the men of our families." She batted her lashes. "I am certain you are most protective of your sisters."

Lady Isabelle and Lady Rosalind exchanged a glance, both of them wrinkling their noses. They were still young. Only fifteen and thirteen, respectively. Obviously, they were not as admiring of their elder brother as Lady Helen.

Simon only nodded to acknowledge her words, his lips

28

pressed firmly together. Anyone who knew the duke's heir would recognize the man's expression for what it was—regret that he had said anything to bring attention to himself.

"The duke will wish to speak to you about what you saw today," Her Grace said, drawing the conversation back to Andrew, perhaps taking pity on her son's discomfort. "You will stay for dinner tonight, won't you, Sir Andrew?"

"If you like, Your Grace."

Josephine rose from her place on the footstool again. "We are going to the theater afterward, Mama." Though her back was to Andrew, he well knew she meant to dis-invite him from dinner, since they already had the evening scheduled out. Silly girl.

He knew what the duchess would say before she said it.

"Oh, I had nearly forgotten." The duchess turned again to Andrew. "Would you accompany us there, too? I am certain Farleigh would appreciate your company."

Everyone in the family used Simon's honorary title when in company with those who were not family. That was the polite thing to do. Andrew looked to his closest friend, waiting for an indication of whether he wanted an additional person in their box that night. But Simon only raised one eyebrow, an odd talent that the duke had passed down to nearly all his children.

"It would be a pleasure, Your Grace. I will send for my things at once." He noted Josephine's posture, the way her shoulders relaxed. She couldn't be relieved to have him coming, could she?

Had she ever been pleased by the promise of his company before? He had certainly looked forward to spending time with her. On more than one occasion. And, of late, he'd had to take himself to task for such thoughts. They weren't brotherly. They were more than friendly, too. And only the continual reminder that he was Simon's friend, not Josie's, kept him in check.

A baronet had no right to more than friendship with a duke's daughter.

Simon gestured to the door. "Come, I will give you the loan of my desk for your note writing." The triumphant gleam in Simon's eyes spoke more than words could of his relief to be away from the ladies and the two guests.

The men bowed to take their leave, and Andrew caught Josephine watching him, her dislike for him glittering in her eyes. His fanciful thoughts were nothing more than daydreams. She didn't care whether he joined them so much as she cared about their verbal sparring. Very well. Before the day was through, they would come to battle, as they always did.

He quite enjoyed their verbal duels, and if that's all he could hope for, he rather looked forward to the next one.

# CHAPTER 4

His Grace, the Duke of Montfort, had sat quietly at the dinner table. Josephine watched him carefully as Sir Andrew told the brief tale of three men entering the Burlington Arcade. She tried, and failed, to guess at her father's thoughts as he contemplated the irate men's intrusion in a place they need not be.

"You did the right thing," he said when Andrew finished speaking, and the rest of the family kept eating their dinner. "Doubtless, many of the people there were frightened."

"Those men had to have known the Arcade would be full of ladies at that time of day. Unprotected ladies." Andrew glanced in Josephine's direction long enough for her to wrinkle her nose at him. "They were cowards," Andrew added, looking back at the duke.

Simon dropped his fork and leaned back in his chair. "I received a letter from my friend in York, Lord Hartwell. He told me there were Luddite uprisings that began as what we are seeing now. General disquiet. A few brazen attacks in the light of day."

"The last time anyone acted against machinery was years ago," Josephine said quickly, bringing everyone's attention to her.

Andrew watched as she sunk slightly in her seat. "It was in Derbyshire."

"So it was," her father said. "But using the word 'last' might be premature. What we see happening in London—indeed, across the country—at this moment could be another branch of that same disquiet and dissatisfaction. The working class face hardship, Josephine. A hardship that empties their pockets without filling their children's bellies." He motioned to the array of food before them. "The cost of food has risen. They see no relief coming, especially in places where there are no members of Lords or Commons to represent their difficulties to the government. The people are angry, but I believe they are as much afraid."

Silence descended upon the table until the dowager duchess sighed. "Things started this way in France, too. Years and years before you children were born."

"Surely we are not as despotic as our neighbors across the Channel," Simon muttered.

"It only takes a few people in power to shift the opinions of the masses," the dowager declared grimly.

The duke sighed, deeply, the sound matching his mother's in a way that linked them as parent and child. "Mother. We are not going to have an English revolution. Not yet."

"You cannot say that," the dowager argued, "when you do not know. These—these radicals want nothing more than to see men such as you brought low, Montfort."

"I believe they want fair representation and fair laws," the duke said, his voice steady and low. "And I believe they should have them. Unfortunately, there are too many people who believe the opposite, and too few willing to discuss ideas of how it might be done."

Before the quiet after that pronouncement became too uncomfortable, the duchess cleared her throat. "I am all for discussing politics as a family so that we might all understand what you work at in Lords, my dear. But I think we had better speak of something more cheerful. Isabelle, will you tell your father about your idea for a garden party?"

The second of the duke's daughters immediately perked up as she began to explain her idea for a party of young people, not yet out in Society, that might gather to come to know one another better before taking their first steps into the adult world in the coming years. Andrew tuned out her cheerful explanations, thinking instead on what the duke had said.

Simon leaned to the side, muttering to Andrew, "Lord Hartwell also told me they are seeing the same unrest in York. The laws forcing our people to buy British grain are hurting more than helping, in his opinion."

Andrew gave a nod of understanding. "Have they had any demonstrations yet? Now that the law against public gathering has expired, I am surprised we are not seeing mass gatherings again. But perhaps it is only because we are in London?"

"He did not mention such a thing." Simon poked at his dinner, his expression darkening. "I don't like what happened today. If you hadn't been there—"

"Sterling had your sister's safety well in hand," Andrew said easily. "No one came to harm."

Simon nodded once, then exhaled sharply. "I hope the play tonight is less taxing than the last time we went to the theater."

"What happened the last time?" Andrew asked, feigning innocence and eliciting a glare from his best friend. "Oh, you mean that little matter with Lady Marchbank?" Simon's frown darkened, and it took some effort for Andrew to not laugh aloud.

On Andrew's other side, Josephine leaned closer. She had obviously overheard them. "If that woman flirts with Simon during the whole play a second time, I will throw my opera glasses at her."

Andrew snorted, drawing a few eyes his way before they drifted back to the duke and duchess discussing the merits of their younger daughter's idea. "Why stop at the glasses?" he asked, looking at her from the corner of his eye. "Let us hurl a chair in her direction and see if she understands the message."

Simon looked heavenward as though for rescue from their ridiculousness. Josephine covered a laugh. And Andrew sat comfortably between them, as he always had, quite at home with the family and his place in their lives.

THE REST OF DINNER PASSED UNEVENTFULLY. JOSEPHINE didn't want to speak another minute about the *incident*. Though plays were not her favorite form of entertainment, she did not mind spending the evening watching as actors and actresses danced across a stage in clever costumes if it meant they could simply move on and talk of something else.

Emma loved theatricals, which gave Josephine good reason to pay attention during this one. She intended to write her friend a letter all about the evening and direct it to the embassy. Every day brought Emma and the count closer to returning to London, and then Josephine would finally have someone to tell about her publishing disappointment.

Perhaps Emma could read the manuscript and offer a helpful critique. What if the problem with her story had to do with the romantic plot? Perhaps she hadn't written the heroine's love for the hero in believable enough terms.

"She really ought to throw him over, don't you think?" Andrew whispered from behind Josephine.

She startled from her thoughts and turned around, glaring at him in the semi-darkness. "I beg your pardon?"

Andrew's laughing eyes flashed at her in the darkness. "The lady in the play. I cannot even remember her name. It seems all the characters are named John or Mary."

Josephine looked to the stage again and at last paid attention to the actress lamenting her lover's lack of care for her heart. "Throw him over?"

"Jilt him," Andrew whispered, closer now. Josephine looked behind her to see that the dratted man had moved his chair closer to hers. He was practically breathing down her neck, causing bumps to rise along her arms. Thankfully, her gloves covered any evidence of such a silly thing.

"A brief neglect is no reason to end a promising romance," Josephine said from behind her fan, barely turning her head so he might hear.

Simon sat next to Andrew. The duchess and duke occupied the other two chairs at the front of the private box, but they were huddled together, the duke's arm around the back of the duchess's chair, likely whispering to one another.

The deep chuckle behind her almost made Josephine shiver. "You cannot tell me you would suffer a man who proclaimed love one moment, only to ignore you completely the next."

"Is that what's going on?" Simon's voice asked. "I hoped they'd killed the fellow off."

Josephine turned fully in her seat to subdue them both with her frown. "Hush. You are both terrible distractions." She turned around again, making a greater effort to pay attention to the mournful heroine, now joined by a matron in the costume of a nun. Apparently, the heroine had been promised to the Catholic church and would be forced to give up her true love if he did not come for her in time.

A rather awful fate, perhaps, but not any worse than sitting through the overly melancholy play itself.

Andrew spoke in her ear again. "I think the convent is a better option for her at this point."

"Nonsense." Josie gritted her teeth. The hero had appeared on stage again, swaggering and boasting about coming into his inheritance. "See, he can afford to marry her now."

"They could both afford it before," he pointed out. "He didn't like that she outranked him. Ridiculous."

Though she privately agreed, Josephine shook her head and kept speaking over her shoulder. "They are going to wed and live happily henceforth."

"Until he neglects her again in favor of some other wild scheme." Andrew lightly poked her arm above her glove, the soft material of his glove warm against her skin. "You would not put up with it, Josie. Admit it."

She curled her hands into fists. She had told Andrew more times than she could count that he could not call her that anymore. Since her presentation at court, even her family rarely used their pet name for her. "Lady Josephine," she reminded him.

"Sir Andrew," he said in return. "Though you should know, we are already well acquainted."

The bothersome man! Perhaps she ought to throw her opera glasses at *him*. Of course, that might damage the beautiful accessory her father had gifted her the year she entered Society. So instead, she took her fan in hand, turned around, and shook it at him in as threatening a manner as she could.

"Will you *please* be silent while I enjoy the play?"

"The play that just ended, you mean?" he asked, eyes twinkling and grinning like a tiger.

"What?" She turned around just as the hero clasped the heroine to him, saying something about eternal love, and then the applause began. Her mouth fell open, and she turned around, ready to berate Andrew, only to find him laughing at her while clapping his hands.

Drat him. He had made her miss the ending and whatever speech of love the principal characters had given each other. That would be one less thing to write in her letter to Emma.

She stood and gave his shoulder a hard whack with her fan—which did absolutely no damage to him, nor made any impact on the others in their box. The duke and duchess were already speaking to an acquaintance the next box over, and Simon stood at the back of their box speaking to the manservant waiting for them. All but one guardsman remained outside the theater, because His Grace, Simon, and Andrew were with them that evening.

Andrew stood, his height making him half-a-head taller than she. "Your fan is not a suitable weapon, Josie. Maybe you ought to carry a stick like your brother."

"If I did, I would run you through with the concealed blade," she promised. "Why must you always be so vexing?"

"Me? Vexing?" He placed a hand upon his chest, eyes widening with comic confusion. "I am told I am quite charming."

"Agitating," she said in return. "Disagreeable, and provoking. That is what you are."

"Provoking?" His grin returned, one side of his mouth going higher than the other as he leaned toward her. "And what is it that I *provoke* from you, *Lady* Josephine?"

Why was he standing so close? And why did he have to be so tall? She stood on her toes to answer him, bringing them nearly nose-to-nose as she hissed, "Exasperation, *Sir* Andrew."

His lips tightened to conceal his smile, though that one side remained tilted upward. His eyes sparkled at her, his amusement making her cheeks grow warm as a strange, twisting-sort of feeling took hold of her stomach. His gaze momentarily fell from hers and drifted lower to her mouth. Her lips parted, but she could not find another disdain-laden word to say, though she became increasingly aware of the rapid thrum of her pulse.

What was happening?

"Father." Simon's deep voice interrupted her thoughts, and she quite suddenly remembered they were in public, where anyone might see her behaving like a child.

She stepped away at the same moment Andrew turned to look at her brother.

Simon's expression was more somber than usual. "There is a

disturbance outside the theater. Rockwell says a small crowd has gathered across the street. We should go. Now."

Her father rose from his seat, taking leave from the people he and her mother had been chatting with since the play's end. His face was a mask of confidence, and her mother's was just as poised.

Josephine swallowed back her nerves and stepped forward to follow them—only to stop when Andrew offered her his arm. "Let Simon and Rockwell take up the rear."

Simon had his walking stick. Rockwell carried a long knife and a concealed pistol. It made sense to have them at the back of the party. She nodded and accepted Andrew's arm. As much as they bickered, she trusted him the same as her father trusted him.

He would keep her safe.

Andrew drew Josephine along with him, keeping her close by tucking his arm to his side. He didn't have time to think on what had happened in the box. How near he'd come to—what? Kissing her? No. Of course that wasn't where their debate would lead. And there was certainly no use following that line of thought.

He kept one eye on the duke and the other on their surroundings as he followed His Grace and Her Grace out of the theater. Perhaps half of the ladies and gentlemen in attendance that night had already spilled from the doors of the theater into the street. There were shouts for carriages, laughter as friends gathered in little circles to talk, and enough chatter to create a din too loud to hear anything clearly.

And it seemed no one except the duke's men were paying any attention to the crowd of men across the street. Some were dressed roughly, others wore the clothing of the middle-class. But they all stared grimly at the theater.

Someone shouted, "Fair representation!"

Another, "No more corn tax!"

And then the chanting started, a variation of both shouts taken up by the men across the street from the theater.

Rockwell, the same age as the duke, looked grim. He signaled with one hand above the crowd and one of his men, Sterling, appeared at the duchess's side.

"It doesn't look like they mean harm, Your Grace," Sterling said to the duke.

"Crowds like this never start off with that aim," Rockwell growled out.

Andrew pulled Josephine closer, and she didn't resist.

"The carriage?" the duke asked.

"Front of the line, Your Grace," Sterling said. "Penn and Hunt are waiting there." Andrew recognized the names of two other men-at-arms trained to protect the ducal family.

He looked down at Josephine to see her face had gone white. His heart squeezed at the fear in her eyes, and he reassured her with gentleness. "A few angry shouts, Josie. Nothing more. We'll be safe in the carriage in no time."

Her face turned upward, and that strange flicker of warmth in his chest returned. He'd felt it moments ago in the box, when she'd looked ready to throttle him for his nettlesome behavior. He'd almost dared her to seek her revenge, as curious as he was enter-tained by the idea of what she would say or do if he had goaded her even one step more.

He didn't have time to think on pushing her to continue their battle. Instead, he put all his thoughts into something more impor-tant—keeping her safe.

Together, their small party wound their way through the theater-goers, who had grown quiet as they listened to the chanting across the street. If everyone remained calm, the constables would arrive and disperse the crowd peacefully. The people dressed in their evening finery would get into their carriages and go home, the evening's entertainment still fresh in their minds.

Except someone on the theater-side of the street shouted, a male voice carrying to those on the other side, "Do they think any of us care?"

Scattered, nervous laughter followed the shout. But the people protesting their government's disregard seemed to snarl as one. The shouting started, back and forth across the street, and Andrew's heart raced as he kept Josephine with him. Someone stepped on her dress, and she nearly fell to the ground before he caught her up against him.

Her wide blue eyes looked up at him. "What if they mob us?" she asked, voice hoarse with fear.

"I'll look after you," he promised, raising his eyes to see that their pause had separated them from the duke, duchess, and Sterling.

Rockwell appeared on Josephine's other side. "You all right, my lady?"

She nodded tensely, and then Simon was there too. The four of them pushed forward and in another blessed minute burst free of the crowd. The duke's conveyance was there, and Sterling held the door open. The duke and duchess were already inside.

Andrew handed Josephine in, then waited for Simon to climb in with his family before he did the same.

The duke, duchess, and Josephine sat on the forward-facing seat, Josephine between her parents and as white as bone china. Her mother had her arm around her eldest daughter, murmuring soothingly in her ear. The duke appeared grim. "This cannot go on long before there is violence," he said, the prediction ominous.

Andrew and Simon, on the rear-facing seat, shared a glance. The duke had spoken to them of what he planned should the situation in London not get any better.

"You must all return to Clairvoir," His Grace declared, and the carriage jolted as it moved away from the theater and its angry crowd. "I will not have my family endangered by the unrest in London."

Andrew looked to Josephine, noting her wide eyes, and the dazed expression upon her face. His heart lurched protectively, and his hands tightened into fists at his side. She hadn't come to harm, he reminded himself. And the duke would ensure her future safety.

The concern for her kept hold of his thoughts, and he had to turn from her to stare out the dark window and the gas lamps of London. A moment had passed between them in the theater, amid their usual sort of argument. When Josephine had looked at him with laughter in her eyes and a smile upon her lips. He had very nearly... No. He hadn't done anything. Hadn't thought anything. He had simply admired her smile.

Things had become increasingly more difficult for Andrew in regards to Josephine. When he returned with Simon from Ireland the year before, he'd seen Josephine anew. She wasn't merely Simon's little sister anymore. She was a woman grown. A beautiful woman, with a sharp intellect. And he'd had to squash all other admiring thoughts of her to avoid traveling down a path he had no right to tread.

Better not to dwell on that when there were more serious matters at hand. And when friendship with Simon, admiration for her father, and his own status as a mere baronet, kept any feeling other than concern for Josephine's well-being at bay.

No one said another word. Not even when they arrived safely again at Dinard House. Because the Duke of Montfort always had the last say when it came to his family's well-being.

# CHAPTER 5

S omehow, Josephine's mother convinced the duke that she had to remain in London with him. But when Josie dared ask if she might remain with her mother, thinking of seeing Emma upon her friend's return to London, the duchess refused to even consider such a thing.

"It is one thing for me to remain here, to support my husband as he fights the prejudices of Parliament," her mother said sternly, watching as Josephine's maid packed her trunk. "It is another to keep our children cooped up in a London house when they might instead be safely in the country, enjoying the freedom of our castle and grounds."

Though Josephine understood her parents' concerns, sending her away struck her as patently unfair.

Thus, the dowager duchess, Josephine, Isabelle, Rosalind, and their governess were packed into a carriage. Lord James, her youngest sibling, was away at school and would join them at the castle when their parents did. The duke sent Simon with them. Their eldest brother kept pace on his horse outside the carriage, under orders from their father to watch over the needs of the family and castle.

Why Sir Andrew had to come, too, Josephine could not guess. Yet there he was, on the morning of their departure, astride his favorite butter-yellow mare and wearing a grin as though they embarked on an adventure rather than a retreat.

Once they were out of London, the carriage maintained a steady speed. Servants and baggage had been sent ahead to their first stop along the way. They would first stay at an estate near Hitchin, a mere forty miles north of the city proper. Then they would travel another fifty miles to Peterborough and finally arrive home at Clairvoir Castle, the family's ancestral seat on the border of Leicestershire and Rutland.

Josephine sat in the forward-facing seat next to her grandmother. Her sisters sat on either side of their governess opposite. The long journey, normally made with the entire family, was as monotonous as it was familiar.

At the end of the first leg, they arrived at the home of a family friend who was presently residing in London. When the dowager duchess traveled, she never stayed at inns. They had enough acquaintances and relatives in England to make that a surety.

"The Barrington servants have been instructed to see to our needs and provide fresh horses for tomorrow," Josephine's grandmother reminded them as they turned up the lane to the Earl of Barrington's country house. "I expect the three of you ladies to conduct yourselves as befitting your father's title. Give the servants nothing to gossip about."

"Yes, Grandmama," all three of them, including Josie, chorused.

When the carriage stopped at the beautiful house, Josephine peered out the window. The sun would sink in a matter of hours, keeping her in the house with the others until she could turn in for the night. She couldn't wander about the Barrington house when they were not home, so she would likely be trapped in the same room with her grandmother, sisters, brother, and Sir Andrew.

The carriage door opened, and Simon appeared, his usual

stoic smile in place as he held his hand out to the dowager duchess. "Grandmother. I hope the trip was not too taxing for you."

"Too taxing?" She took his hand and stepped out. "Young man, when the day comes that a simple carriage ride is *taxing* on me, I will go to my grave. I would hazard a guess that you will regret the day's travel more than I."

Simon cast an amused glance back at Josephine as he escorted their grandmother to the front doors.

Andrew took Simon's place, his hand outstretched to Josephine. In precedence, she came next. She did not hesitate to accept his help out of the carriage. They had known one another too long, and many situations had forced him to play her escort over the years.

A footman would help her sisters and governess from the carriage, and they would make their path up the steps of the house unescorted.

For all his hours in the saddle, Andrew appeared remarkably chipper. "How did you pass the hours today, my lady?" he asked. "Reading poetry to one another? Embroidery?"

"Mostly in pleasant conversation," she answered him. "Not that you would know much about such things."

"Are you implying I am unable to converse intelligently?" he asked, a challenge in his voice.

"Of course not." She smiled, keeping her voice light and pleasant as they started up the steps into the house. "I know of your intelligence and would not insult it. It is the pleasing nature of the conversation that you would know nothing of, since speaking with you is often a trial of patience."

He chuckled, and she frowned. Her dart had missed the mark, as it so often did with him. She amused him, while he exasperated her. They were forever on uneven footing in their verbal sparring matches. Someday, she would get the upper hand.

Thankfully, they parted company soon enough, and Josephine

retired to her guest room until dinner. Susan, her maid, had gone ahead with the other personal servants and their trunks, leaving Josie alone until she rang for a maid to help her prepare for the evening meal.

She ought to have read. Or written a letter. Or done something productive. Instead, she laid down upon the bed and stared up at the canopy. Thinking through the story she had written, from beginning to end.

The tale wasn't too unlike those that she had read before. She wrote about a poor gentlewoman who lived with a spinster aunt, detailing her place in village society. Her heroine dutifully helped others yet experienced little kindness herself. Until a handsome vicar appeared and noticed her efforts, then fell deeply in love with her.

Josephine thought it a perfect story. But then, mothers often thought her children perfect, without full awareness of their flaws. But where had she gone wrong? It was a tale with a moral. Kindness and gentleness of heart was rewarded fairly. There was an element of romance and prior tragedy.

The room grew dark before Josephine found a satisfactory answer to her problem. Alas, she summoned a maid and prepared for dinner no closer to a solution than when she'd arrived.

THOUGH ANDREW WOULD NEVER ADMIT IT, GIVEN HIS LOVE for horses and riding, Simon's grandmother was right. He sunk into a hot tub of water in the dressing room provided for his use and sighed with gratitude. The water was almost hot to the point of discomfort, which meant he'd have extra time to enjoy a soak before having to dress for dinner.

Dressing for dinner in the middle of a journey struck him as somewhat unnecessary, but Her Grace, the dowager duchess, was insistent that they maintain the strictest of standards. He had the greatest respect for the woman, but he'd gladly forgo dressing in stiff formality for the comfort of eating alone in his room.

Andrew did not leave his tub until the water cooled and his muscles protested. As he dressed for dinner, his eye caught on the small narrow box in his trunk. The box that held the pen he'd purchased for Josephine—an impulsive thing to do, surely. If they'd all stayed in London, he could have presented it to her at the family dinner given in honor of her birthday. Now he was carting it about with him. Somehow, that made the gift seem ridiculous.

Why had he bothered with it in the first place?

He dressed quickly and left his room, despite the early hour, and went in search of Simon.

He found the duke's eldest son and heir in the sitting room adjoining the dining room. The only public room designated for the family's use during their one evening at the estate.

Simon wasn't using the sitting room to sit. He was marching from one side of the room to the other. In his hand, he held his stylized walking stick, which concealed a blade longer that Andrew's forearm.

"Are you pacing or patrolling?" Andrew leaned against the doorway. "Sterling is in the hall. Would you like to change guard positions with him?"

His friend stopped mid-stride and looked at the closed door. "Sometimes, I think I might enjoy his place more than my own." He took up his stick in both hands, looking down at the wood casing with furrowed brow. "Do you think my father overreacted by sending us away?"

Andrew tipped his head to the side, studying his friend and trying to determine what the other man needed to hear. "I have rarely questioned your father's motives for anything. While I know he isn't infallible, I have yet to see evidence of it."

Simon twisted the top of his walking stick and drew the blade a few inches from its casing. The metal caught the candlelight and reflected the soft orange glow. "I have trained all my life to defend myself, and we have discussed as a family what to do if one of us is ever held for ransom. We have contingency plans for everything. Secret rooms. Hidden caches of funds. As a boy, I thought for certain we would never have need of any of it. Now." He re-sheathed the blade completely and tucked the stick beneath his arm. "Now I almost wish we would, if only to justify all that training."

"Understandable." Andrew pushed away from the door and went to one of the overstuffed sofas. "Yet I have heard your father say that it is better for a man of peace to prepare for war than to only hope it never comes to that."

"You needn't quote my own father to me." Simon's smile was slight, but it was amused. "I could fill a book with his proverbs." He went to the fireplace and laid his stick atop the hearth. "I wish he had let me stay in London. Sending me as escort to Grand-mother and my sisters wasn't exactly subtle."

"You're the heir." Andrew shrugged. "Tucking you away safe and sound is habit by now."

Simon exhaled sharply. "Habit or not, I could have helped in London."

Though Andrew didn't presume to know the mind of a duke, he did know his friend well enough to recognize him wallowing in self-pity. "Your father has more help than he needs. And besides that, did you ever think he didn't send you to get you out of harm's way, so much as because he trusts you with the well-being of the people he loves most?"

"What do you mean? The girls?"

"Of course. Your sisters mean the world to the duke and duchess. They send your grandmother for propriety's sake, then they send you because they trust you to look after things in their absence." Andrew smirked and leaned back, folding his arms over his chest. "Your father is a lion of a man. He would never leave his daughters without protection."

Though Simon said nothing to that, he appeared thoughtful. Finally, he said, "Have I thanked you for joining us?"

"Not properly." Andrew grinned, and prepared to say more, but the door opened.

Sterling, dressed in the plain clothing of a servant, waited for Lady Josephine to enter before closing the door behind her. Andrew rose, as was polite. She came into the room dressed for dinner, her hair arranged simply with a handful of pearls peeking out from beneath her dark curls. She looked from Simon to Andrew, and he noted the tension in her expression with interest.

"Grandmama and the girls are not down yet?"

"As you see," Simon said, gesturing to the empty seats. "They only left to prepare for dinner a quarter hour ago. Grandmother lamented that you did not join us earlier, so be prepared for her to bring that up."

Her eyebrows pinched together above the bridge of her nose. "Oh, bother. I did not think anyone would mind if I rested alone. We spent all of today talking." She settled on the opposite end of Andrew's couch, allowing him to retake his seat.

"I recall you mentioning that before," Andrew said, slanting a smile in her direction. "You said it was pleasant. How could you not wish for more of the same?"

With her posture absolutely perfect, Josephine turned her head to give him the benefit of her full attention. "Have you never heard of moderation in all things, Sir Andrew?"

"Certainly. I studied the Greek poets along with your brother. But I doubt you mean to avoid more time with your grandmother in order to appease some sort of philosophical goal." He settled more comfortably in his seat, and she immediately stiffened. "What have you been doing all this time? I might presume a nap, except you still carry a look of fatigue about you."

She narrowed her dark blue eyes at him. "One should not insult a lady by saying she looks *tired*, Sir Andrew. Your studies are lacking if you think that is acceptable." She folded her hands in her lap and twisted her ring about her finger. "I was resting."

Andrew looked to Simon, who he found staring at him with one raised eyebrow—the duke's trick he had passed on to all his children. That simple gesture could mean a multitude of things, and the duke himself used it to great advantage. At the moment, Simon seemed to convey his amusement.

"It is a pity you must ride in that carriage all day," Simon said. "Even if you enjoy the conversation as much as Andrew says you do."

Josephine's smile was brief and faltering. "I know. If only the two of you had brought a carriage, too. I might have switched from one to the other when the enjoyable conversation grew too taxing."

The duke had kept their second family conveyance in town, for his eventual return to Clairvoir Castle with their mother.

Something more bothered Josephine than her time spent in the carriage. Andrew could sense it. But was it only her fatigue? He saw evidence of that easily enough. "Would you prefer to ride?" he asked, trying to tease another reaction from her. "I will trade my seat atop Honey for one in the carriage, if you wish."

"If I thought you were the least bit serious, I might take you up on the idea." Her lips tightened into a smile. "Though I suppose riding side-saddle all day would have its own unpleasantness."

"Riding astride certainly does," Simon muttered on the other side of the room.

Josephine's smile melted away. "Do you think Papa and Mama will be all right in London? If there really is danger for us there, how can they stay?"

"It depends on what happens next, Josie." Simon folded his arms, turning to face his sister fully, his expression stern. "If father has fewer family members to worry over, his concentration can turn to Parliament and making things better. With all of us in Town, coming and going as we please, he could never be certain we were safe. Especially if crowds like the one at the theater keep gathering."

"No one has been hurt yet," Andrew added. "But it's only a matter of time until tempers grow too hot, or someone grows too impatient."

"Precisely." Simon paced to the window, looking out to the darkness beyond. "Returning to Clairvoir is the best thing we can do for Father."

Josephine nodded, the movement slow and thoughtful. Then she turned to look at Andrew again. "And why, precisely, are you joining us in our exile? Are you bored with the Season already?"

"Absolutely." He grinned at her. "It's always the same, isn't it? The same balls, the same sitting rooms, the same gossip? I feel certain I will miss nothing, though many will likely miss my company." He dangled that statement for her, as a challenge, waiting for her to pounce upon his words and declare him arrogant or refute his claim altogether.

Instead, Josephine gave another weak nod. Then she studied her hands again without saying a word to him. "I do hope Mama is all right. Her days will be long and lonely if she stays at the house, waiting for Papa to come home every evening." Her words drifted into quiet.

The next moment brought her sisters into the room, dressed for dinner and chatting amiably with each other about their rooms. Josephine's expression changed to something that held more warmth, but her eyes kept that tired and pinched look about them. He looked to Simon to see if the future duke noticed Josephine's distress, but Simon's eyes had already dimmed, likely with his own concerns.

The dowager duchess joined them a few minutes later, and Andrew tried not to worry over Josephine. Instead, he turned his efforts to making her younger sisters giggle and her grandmother pretend to be unamused by his antics. But when he escorted

Josephine to dinner, the wan smile she gave him brought his concerns to the forefront of his mind.

Was she only concerned about her father and mother? Perhaps Emma's absence made everything more potent for Josephine. She had never been without a friend with Emma as her companion. Andrew did not nettle her as he usually did. Instead, he watched and studied, and wondered if there was more he ought to do.

# CHAPTER 6

Three days of travel, crowded together in a carriage, and in unvarying company, couldn't be pleasant. When Andrew stood at the open carriage door, hand extended for Josephine, he saw the weariness in her eyes as she placed her gloved hand in his. Simon walked ahead with his grandmother, and the dowager duchess was already snapping out instructions to the staff who had gathered to welcome them in the vestibule.

Josephine gave him a somewhat pained smile. "I think I would have preferred riding," she whispered.

Andrew reflexively squeezed the slim fingers in his grasp before tucking her hand into the crook of his arm. The moment she had settled her hand in the familiar spot, the tension in his shoulders relaxed. He walked down the long corridor lined with ancient swords and weaponry. Clairvoir Castle welcomed everyone the same—with an assurance of protection and reminders of prestige.

They came into the first hall, the black and white marble floor glistening and the two hearths on either side of the room blazing with warmth and light. Simon stood at the bottom of the first set of stairs that led upward to a split, where it diverged in opposite directions. Her Grace, the dowager duchess, had gone ahead with the housekeeper at her heels.

Simon had just handed his hat and gloves to a manservant. "I see you are relatively unscathed from our travels, Sister."

Josephine released her hold on Andrew to strip her gloves from her hands and give them to a maid. "Except for the dust, which I will see to directly," she murmured.

Isabelle and Rosalind came in, arm in arm. "I am so glad we are home," Isabelle declared, wearing a wide grin. "Another day in the carriage with Grandmama would have been awful."

"Lady Isabelle," her governess rebuked softly from behind her. Mrs. Robinson, a practical woman, shared a wan smile with Josephine. "Come, ladies. We must get you to your rooms so you can prepare for dinner."

Rosalind groaned aloud. "I would rather skip dinner and go straight to bed for a fortnight." She looked the least like her parents of all her siblings. Her hair had lightened as she aged, and her eyes were brown rather than the vivid blue Josephine shared with her other siblings and her mother.

"You weren't the one Grandmama asked to read Italian poetry," Isabelle muttered as they followed Mrs. Robinson up the stairs. "I will never forgive Emma for giving Grandmama that book. She *knew* we would be the ones reading it aloud."

Josephine covered her mouth and looked to Simon, who returned her look of mirth with a weary smile of his own.

Andrew pushed his hand through his hair, finally devoid of his hat. "Italian poetry. That must have kept the lot of you entertained."

"Careful, Sir Andrew," Josephine warned. "You know Grandmama likes it when you read to her, too."

"I cannot help that I have the perfect reading voice and cadence." He puffed his chest out and pretended to flick dust from a shirtsleeve. "I am in great demand as a reader."

"You, sir, are highly pompous about your talents." Josephine smirked and walked to the steps, saying over her shoulder, "However few you may possess."

Andrew hid his smile as she ascended the stairs and turned out of view, going to the family wing where she would rest and prepare for the evening meal. He turned to Simon. "Someday, your sister will admit she likes me." Though he said it in jest, he wondered.

His oldest friend raised both eyebrows but said nothing, only gestured for the two of them to follow after everyone else. They had climbed both sets of stairs before Simon spoke, his tone serious. "Thank you for coming with me, Andrew."

"You need to stop expressing your gratitude, or I'll start to think I deserve it." Andrew laughed. "You're too eager to thank me for something I eagerly volunteered for. What would I do in London without you? You are the reason I get invited to the best parties and balls, for one thing. For another, I would rather spend a fortnight at Clairvoir than any amount of time anywhere else. Including my own estate."

Simon chuckled, the first sign of lightness he'd shown since they'd mounted their horses that morning. His shoulders sagged as much as Andrew had ever seen them. "It is good to be home."

The castle was that for all of them. Home. Even Andrew could not think of a place where he felt as at ease and content— which might be the reason he preferred to stay at the castle rather than journey back and forth from his estate in Bytham.

As he went through the motions of preparing for dinner, he reflected on why that was. The easy answer was also the truest one—Bytham Castle was lonely. His family had possessed the old house for two centuries, but parts of the building had stood for four. Perhaps it had once been beautiful, but now it felt cold and ancient.

He had often thought about selling it and establishing a new house for future generations. When he'd mentioned the idea in front of the duchess, Her Grace had been quite vocal about reconstruction rather than abandonment. Something that she knew how to do well, considering she had turned the old castle into what it was now.

Andrew had neither her patience nor her passion for such work. Not to mention funds. He had enough to live quite comfortably, with an income from his father's investments that promised to keep the family living well for generations to come. But the blunt it would take to pull apart a building and put a new one together in its place would take far more ready money than Andrew had.

Dinner that evening was a quiet affair, though everyone came to the table as the dowager duchess expected. Andrew felt the tension in Josephine, so he decided he'd grant her a reprieve. He turned his attention to teasing her younger sisters instead.

After dinner, rather than the ladies going to the sitting room and the men sitting about with port, everyone agreed to turn in for bed.

"It is time to accustom ourselves to country hours again," the dowager declared with a firm nod. "Early to bed, and early to rise."

"Are we allowed to visit our friends?" Isabelle asked as everyone stood from the table. "To let everyone know we've returned to the neighborhood."

Simon gave his young sister a tired smile. "Father said we could carry on as normal, just so long as you take one of the footmen with you if you leave the grounds."

"Must we declare our return so soon?" Josephine asked, shooting her grandmother a pained look. "The moment people know we are in residence we will receive invitations. I should like a few days to recover first."

"It will not be too much, I think, given that your parents are still in London." The dowager sniffed. "Our neighbors of the most social consequence remain in London, too. And for those who are about...well. It is not as though we can keep our arrival secret."

She gestured to the lights blazing along the walls and the servants standing at the ready.

Andrew followed the family to their wing of the house. His was the only guest room in that quarter, the rest were across the castle to allow the family privacy from their visitors. Likely to offer a buffer for them, too. The servants had found more than one young lady searching for the heir's chambers during house parties.

"Tomorrow, we should *not* go riding," Simon said as they passed the doors of the ladies' rooms. "I have no wish to sit on a horse for the rest of the week."

"How dreadfully dull of you." Andrew stopped before Simon's room and looked down the hall as the last door closed behind one of the girls. "You know that is my favorite way to pass the time. If you are to take that from me, whatever will I do with myself?"

"Make trouble, most likely." Simon waved him away. "Leave me be. We'll find a way for you to fritter away your hours in the morning."

"We both know you will be elbow-deep in estate business before noon." Andrew kept walking, going to his room. "Never fear. You needn't entertain me. I will find a way to occupy myself."

"Torturing Josephine, most likely."

Andrew hesitated, a few steps away from his door still. "It isn't really torture, you know." Although Andrew couldn't himself put another name to it.

In the flickering light of the corridor, Simon's eyebrow arched much like his father's when the duke wished to drive a point deeper. "I am aware there is more to your bickering than that. Are you?"

Worry pricked his conscience. He wouldn't risk their friendship or his place in the family by complicating things. "Josephine is like a sister to me. As she has always been."

"Of course." His friend stepped into his own room. "Good night, Andrew." He heard Simon's chuckle as the door closed.

Andrew's bedroom was dark, the embers in his hearth glowing softly, and the chamber felt rather hollow. Quite a lot of things felt empty, these days. Whenever Andrew was alone, he wished to be anywhere else. With anyone else.

Andrew had noticed his valet appeared as exhausted as everyone else when he'd readied Andrew for dinner. Poor fellow. He'd given him the rest of the evening off.

Rather than completely undress, he took off his coat and tossed it over a chair. Then he knelt by the fire and built it up until it crackled, the sound cheery in the too-silent room. Then he lit a lamp beside his bed, and finally started pacing from one side of the room to the other. Restless.

He might ache all over from three and a half days in the saddle, but a good meal and familiar environment had perked him up. Sleep would not come quickly, but with everyone else in the house turning in, what was he to do?

A small collection of books waited upon the shelf in his room. They were volumes he had purchased while staying with the family and left at the castle rather than take them home. He picked up the stack and brought the books with him to the chair pulled up near the fireplace. He read one spine after another, putting each down on the table at his elbow, before settling with the last volume. Ah, yes. The novel his cousin had gifted him shortly before her marriage.

*The Bravo of Venice, A Romance.*

His cousin had thought it delightful because the whole book had been written by a German, translated into English, and surely bore no resemblance to Venice as it existed. He settled into his chair, pulled off his shoes, and put his stockinged feet up on a padded stool. He sank into the story the way he had earlier lowered himself into his tub—expecting nothing but relaxation.

The story of a bandit and assassin in disguise soon pulled him in. He was thoroughly enjoying every word, and he reached the conversation between the heroine and her governess with a grin on his face.

*Who was talking about husbands?* the young heroine asked. *What I feel for Flodoardo is merely affection, friendship.*

Andrew saw through that as easily as the governess did. And he suddenly wondered if Josephine had read this book yet. She would enjoy it, he felt certain. She always had interesting views on women in fiction. What would she think about this self-denying heroine?

Before he could get farther in the characters' argument, he heard a noise in the corridor. He reflexively turned to look under the seam where his door nearly met the floor and saw at once the soft glow of light.

Someone was out of bed.

He looked at the mantel clock. He'd been reading for half an hour. It wasn't entirely late yet, but with everyone else gone to sleep...

Andrew left his book on the chair and went to peer out into the hall, curious as to which family member was creeping about in the near-dark. And why. If it was one of the younger girls, he'd do the family a favor and point her right back to where she had come from.

He barely stuck his head out of his room and saw at once the tall, graceful figure of a woman walking softly away from his door. She held a candle aloft in one hand, and a dark shawl covered the bright blue of the gown she had worn to dinner that evening.

"Josie?" he whispered, and she immediately stilled. She slowly turned around. She clutched a rectangular box to her chest with one arm and held a candle with the other.

"Andrew," she whispered back. "I thought everyone had gone to sleep."

He came out into the hall, closing his door behind him. "So

did I." He took a few steps toward her, and she gripped the box she carried tighter. He paused. "What do you have there?"

She swallowed and affected a haughty tone. "That is none of your business."

"Ah." He came closer still and watched with some satisfaction as she tried to cross her other arm over the box, too, the candle flickering as it passed beneath her nose. So. Josephine had a secret. "What could be in that box, I wonder, that brings you out of your room to skulk through the castle like a ghost?"

"I am *not* skulking," she insisted, voice dropping to a quieter tone. "I am perfectly allowed to come and go in this castle as I wish."

"True, but I find it interesting you waited until you thought everyone was asleep to 'come and go' this evening. In truth, you ought to have delayed your suspicious errand another half hour at least. I wager I am not the only one still waiting for sleep to take me. Any moment now, someone else will open their door because they hear us."

She glanced down the corridor, lowering her arm somewhat as she did. "My errand isn't suspicious."

"Your behavior certainly is."

"If I want to take a walk in my family's home—"

"With a box you won't let me see."

"I already told you, the box isn't any of your affair."

"Which only makes me more desirous to discover what is inside."

"It isn't my duty to see to your desire. You should go back to your room, because you will not get any satisfaction from me." She put her nose in the air.

Andrew chuckled. "My dear Josie, you are the very last lady I would look to for the satisfaction of my desires."

Her jaw dropped open, and a gasp of air escaped her. "What did you say?"

He grinned without the least bit of repentance. "I am confident you heard me."

She blustered. "My father would be shocked—"

"Your father would want to know what you're doing in the corridor when you ought to be in bed." He folded his arms, feeling quite superior in that moment.

"Go away," Josephine snapped. She turned and started walking again.

Andrew followed and watched as her shoulders drew up closer and closer to her ears before she spun around again, making the flame of her candle waver dangerously.

"Stop following me."

"I have as much right to walk down this corridor in the dark as you do."

"Then walk the other direction."

"No, I think I would like to see where you are going."

"Without your shoes on?"

He looked down at his feet, then shrugged. "I see no need for shoes. Unless you mean to lead me out of doors?"

She considered him a moment. "You are not going to leave me alone, are you?"

"You know me so well."

"Unfortunately." She glowered at him. "How are you and Emma even related? She is the dearest lady, while you are forever provoking me."

"Emma and I have more in common than you would guess." He looked at the box in her arms again. "We both take an inordinate amount of interest in your doings."

"Well, I wish you would stop."

"I find it far too entertaining to nettle you."

"Why can you not find another person to bother?"

"No one else is sneaking about the castle at the moment."

"You are insufferable."

Andrew shrugged. "You have said so before, Josie. You need to think up new insults."

"Why, when the most ready-to-hand are still accurate?" Her eyes narrowed. "And stop calling me Josie."

"It suits you, though."

"Calling you an imbecile suits, too, but I refrain from such impolite behavior as a general rule." Her eyes blazed with the barb, triumphant at last.

He chuckled, not at all insulted. It had been too long since they'd exchanged words this way. Conversation with Josephine always invigorated him. She kept him sharp, as their wits struck one another the way a knife struck a whetstone. "When you fall to insulting my intelligence, we both know I have won the argument."

"That is entirely false." She scoffed at him, her cheeks full of color and her eyes bright in the candlelight. She enjoyed their verbal jousts as much as he did, even if she never admitted it. "I seriously question your mental acuity with regularity."

"Do you?" He placed a hand over his heart. "But what does that say of your family's efforts to educate me? The duke himself has taken me into his confidence, taught me side-by-side with his son and heir. Perhaps I should report to him that his own daughter finds my intellectual abilities lacking."

She wrinkled her nose at him. "You wouldn't dare bring my father into one of our tiffs."

"I certainly would. Especially as I am certain he would be on my side."

"Andrew—"

"*Sir* Andrew."

A grimace was the last thing he saw on her face before she emitted an irritable huff, which immediately snuffed out the candle. She groaned. "Now look what you made me do."

"My dear Josie, if you wanted to get me alone in the dark—"

Her exasperation came out in a hiss. "The very cheek of the idea."

He had to bite the inside of his cheek to keep from laughing. The only light in the corridor came from the far end, where the stairs to the main part of the house were found. A wall sconce always burned on that end, lighting the way for members of the household should they need to venture out of bed at night. Josephine had gone in the opposite direction.

That flame, far from them as it was, did nothing to illuminate the two of them. Andrew could only make out the barest lines of her form. She would see his outline better, standing as he was between her and the distant light.

He stood aside, leaving her path clear. "Come. Stop your flirting with me, and I'll see you back to your door."

"Flirting with you? Me?" She sounded genuinely shocked at the idea. Proving to him his wishful thinking was only that—a wish she saw more than Simon's bothersome friend when she looked at him.

He needed to stop. Truly. It wasn't fair to him or to her to entertain thoughts of more than whatever it was they already were. Friends? Foes? It didn't matter. Nothing was going to change.

Nor did it matter that, as of late, he had noticed that Josephine blushed when he led their bickering down the path of flirtation, and he quite enjoyed the fluster he caused her. She nearly always gave up when he implied any sort of attraction between them.

"Yes. We both know you find me charming. Secretly."

"Do you like imagining all the women of your acquaintance find you charming? That is the only way I can account for that ridiculous idea."

"Oh?" He stepped closer to her again, watching the movement of her shoulders, the tilt of her head. They were less than an arm's length apart. "Is that truly the only way? Because here we are. In the dark. All alone. Almost as if you willed it so."

"I willed you to leave me alone," she reminded him, her voice dropping to a lower register. "You will recall I wanted nothing to do with you this evening."

"And yet you remain here," he reminded her, leaning closer so he could whisper nearly in her ear. "It is quite scandalous, Josie."

He heard her sharp intake of breath, and his lungs hitched for a moment, clinging to the air inside as he listened to the heavy silence in the corridor. His heartbeat thudded in his ears, almost distracting him from the pleasant scent of Josephine's perfume. Vanilla and roses.

Simon would kill him. Absolutely, without a doubt, run Andrew through with a sword for flirting with his sister. He needed to pull back. And yet, he so often found his teasing with Josephine led to flirtation.

Why couldn't he find someone else to flirt with? Someone who might welcome the attention. He'd never been much of a flirt, though he'd always delighted in debates with intellectual equals. Somehow, with Josephine, those debates were charged differently. Excited him in a way he couldn't explain.

She trod on his foot, her evening slipper soft enough that her step caused no true pain, but the surprise of her movement made him yelp and lurch backward. Then he heard her quick footsteps pass him and return the way they had come. He followed, an apology on his lips.

He had pushed things too far.

Andrew rushed down the corridor, stopping when he collided with the warmth of Josie's form. Her hands flew to his shoulders and his hands wrapped around her waist in an effort to steady them both. She trembled in his grasp, and her breath tickled across his neck.

"Josephine, I'm terribly—"

"Yes," she cut off his hastily prepared speech, sounding somewhat breathless. "You are. And I accept your apology. You are such a nuisance, Andrew." Then she pulled away from him and kept going. He stayed still this time, not wanting to run into her again.

A door opened—hers—letting faint light into the corridor again. She looked over her shoulder at him, and he had one clear view of her profile as she drew herself into the perfect posture of a duke's daughter. "I will say nothing about this evening. I suggest you follow that example." Then she shut the door behind her with such care that he did not hear the moment the latch caught.

Andrew went to his door and slipped inside. He leaned against it for a time, listening to be certain Josephine didn't sneak out again.

All was quiet.

He lost all desire to read. Or to think. Because if he spent too much time thinking, he'd go over the entirety of their conversation again. Because something had happened—or almost happened—in the darkness. He'd felt the stirring in the air between them.

A good night's sleep would banish that line of thinking. He'd worry about Josephine and her mysterious box in the morning. Or, better yet, do his best to forget all about the scene in the corridor.

That seemed the safest course of action. The wisest.

And the most unlikely.

# CHAPTER 7

When Josephine learned that Simon and Andrew had already taken their breakfast, she sat at the table with utter relief. After her failed attempt to sneak her manuscript up to her secret tower, she had no wish to watch Andrew gloat. Though he had thwarted her completely, she would find another time to slip away. She always did.

Castle Clairvoir had several hidden rooms, a few hidden passages, and two secret staircases. They were built into the castle as much for practicality as for the safety of the family. And, Josephine strongly suspected, her mother took a secret delight in hiding things in plain sight.

After she enjoyed her meal alone, Josephine went to the library. Her grandmother would send for her soon, which meant it was best to stay in the main rooms of the house.

She had walked halfway through the library before realizing the door to her father's study—which connected to the library— stood wide open. She heard an unfamiliar voice speaking from inside, too.

"I thought it prudent to come when I learned your family was in residence again. Mr. Gooch left behind notes regarding your castle's chapel. Will you wish for its use for Sunday worship? Or any other services?"

Simon's voice answered with confidence. "I do not think that will be necessary at this time. My father has spoken of using the chapel here, but it doesn't seem all that practical at present."

Josephine drifted nearer to the open door. Mr. Gooch had been a deacon, and then vicar, for their parish for as long as she could remember. Who might this newcomer be, to ask after their religious habits? His voice was pleasant. His accent suggested a more northerly heritage, though educated.

Affecting her most polite, lady-like mask of indifference, Josephine went to the open door and called out, "Farleigh? Are you in father's study?" It was always best to use her brother's title when they were in mixed company.

She came through the doorway as three men rose to their feet —Simon from behind her father's ornate oak desk, Andrew from a chair near the fire, and a third gentleman from the chair across the desk from Simon.

The third man wasn't so tall as her brother—he would only be an inch or so taller than herself. He wore somber, dark-colored clothing with a simple cut and an expression that might have been a match for her own.

"Ah, Josephine." Simon gestured to their visitor. "Allow me to introduce Mr. Jonathan Wood. He is standing as the Lambsthorpe rector while Mr. Gooch visits family in Scotland." Simon then introduced her as his sister, Lady Josephine.

"My lady," the rector said, dark eyes taking her in, his expression somber. "It is a pleasure to meet another member of the esteemed duke's family." He could not be much older than Simon, for all his solemnity.

Josephine came deeper into the room, eyeing the man with some interest. "I did not know Mr. Gooch would be away so long as to necessitate someone else taking his position. How long do you anticipate filling that need at Lambsthorpe, Mr. Wood?"

His dark hair and eyes put her in mind of the hero she had created in her novel. That he shared a vocation with the fictional gentleman also piqued her interest.

"I expect to remain until autumn," he stated with a slight bow of his head. "I am at the archbishop's disposal."

"We are fortunate to have you, Mr. Wood," Simon said in his lordly voice. "I hope you will keep us informed of anything we might do to make your stay in our community more enjoyable and fruitful."

"Thank you, my lord. It was a pleasure to meet you. As well as you, my lady. Sir Andrew." The rector bowed to each of them in turn.

"Are you leaving so soon?" Josephine's mind raced with the possibilities of interviewing the gentleman, though she remained perfectly poised. Years of training as a duke's daughter meant keeping a great many of her emotions to herself. "Allow me to walk you to the foyer, Mr. Wood."

Her back was to Simon, so she did not see his reaction, though she could not miss the way Andrew's eyebrows raised. He needn't act surprised. She was a perfectly polite hostess in her mother's absence. Walking with a new acquaintance down a corridor shouldn't elicit his comment or notice. Yet she felt a challenge in the way Andrew watched her, so Josephine kept her spine as straight as a lightning conductor as she took Mr. Wood's arm at the door.

It wasn't any of Andrew's business how she chose to execute her hostessing duties in her parents' home.

Once out of the library and in the main corridor, Mr. Wood's gaze strayed to the tapestries and paintings on the wall. "Your family's home is quite magnificent, my lady. I understand your mother is responsible for its current design?"

"Yes, she began work on the castle directly after marrying my father. The castle was much plainer in appearance before. There is a model of it my father kept, and I have always found my mother's vision much prettier than the fortress-like block it was before." She paused at the top of the staircase. "Have you seen our chapel, Mr. Wood?"

"I have not yet had that pleasure," he admitted, somewhat less stiffly than before. "Is it anything like what they have at Chatsworth?"

The name of that gloriously large estate had become synonymous with grandeur. As it belonged to another one of England's dukes, Josephine had enjoyed the privilege of staying at Chatsworth on more than one occasion. She was quite familiar with it. "It is not so large, nor so elaborate. But then, we do not have as many visitors at once, not the way the Duke of Devonshire does."

"A shame," he said, "because this part of the country is breathtaking."

She sensed no artifice about him or the compliment to her father's lands. Josephine gestured to a turn in the corridor. "It would also be a shame for you to come all the way up our steep hill and not at least peek in at the chapel. We can step into the family's balcony to save time, if you wish."

The rector hesitated, his dark eyes uncertain. Then he reached inside his coat and drew out a pocket watch on a thin silver chain. Once satisfied with what it told him, he put the watch away and offered his arm to her. "If you would lead the way, my lady, I would like to take advantage of your generous offer."

The entrance to the family's private balcony, tucked away as it was in the same stairwell that servants used regularly, was an assuming arched doorway. Josephine opened the door and entered with the same sense of belonging she felt every time her family held services in the high-ceilinged chamber.

"The family has kept a chapel here for hundreds of years. After the fire that destroyed the old castle, the chapel was restored and embellished to look a bit more gothic. But that painting over the altar has hung here since the seventeenth century, when the eighth Earl of Montfort purchased it in Spain."

The rector stood at the rail, both hands upon it, looking out over the small chapel. "How many people can your family's chapel hold, Lady Josephine?" he asked, his eyes sweeping from the white-arched ceiling down to the black marble floor between the pews.

"I think we have had as many as sixty people here before, at my youngest brother's christening. Father has often said he wishes to use the chapel for regular Sunday meetings."

Mr. Wood's eyebrows arched as he turned to her, and his question stumbled from him, almost as though he did not mean to ask it. "Why has he not yet done so?" His cheeks pinked, and the young priest turned away. He gestured to the room below them. "I mean—of course, it is not my business—I merely meant that the chapel is quite beautiful. It is a shame it is not used regularly."

"You ought to ask my father when he returns." Josephine watched as the man's face went pale, then pinked again. She had been right about him. As stoic as he appeared in her brother's presence, he wasn't a man used to masking his emotions. "I think he would enjoy discussing the possibility with a younger man than Mr. Gooch. Our vicar is wonderful, of course, but he is quite set in his ways. The chapel has been so long out of use that he sees no reason to petition for a new perish."

The rector's brow creased as he turned his attention again to the chapel beneath them. He looked to the tapestries on the walls, then up at the windows which allowed natural light to flood the room. "If you do not think it presumptuous, perhaps I will."

Though she longed to ask the rector a dozen questions about himself, Josephine refrained. She longed to reassure herself of the characterization of her fictional vicar. Instead, she saw Mr. Wood out all the way to the open guardroom, which served as the foyer of the castle. She thanked him for coming, then stood in the center of the room and watched as a footmen led him to the door.

Josephine turned on her heel and happily walked to the steps, already planning her visit to the vicarage, where Mr. Wood lived during his stay. To fix the mistakes of her novel, whatever they were, a better understanding of her hero was in order. What better way to get to know her character than to find someone *real* who was in the same profession and of similar age?

Her good fortune nearly made her forget all about Andrew and the troublesome way he had nearly learned of her secret the night before. She needn't fret about him. Instead, she had to figure out how to slip from the castle without her brother or a guard accompanying her.

When she arrived at the family gallery to meet with her grandmother, Josephine was in the best of moods. Nothing suited her so much as making plans—especially secretive plans.

WATCHING JOSEPHINE FOLLOW THE RECTOR OUT OF THE room had left a strange feeling in Andrew's gut. Not that he thought the gesture anything other than polite. A good hostess would see a single guest to the door, especially one in a position of respect in the clergy. But something had struck him as different in the lady's interaction with Mr. Wood.

Andrew attempted to brush away the feeling. The sensation wasn't entirely gone, however, when he noticed Josephine behaving oddly the next day. He had almost expected her to sneak out of her room again that night and had kept listening for sound in the corridors after everyone went to bed, but there hadn't been so much as a creak on the floor or a rustle of carpet.

But the strange behavior the next day, which only he seemed to notice, made him wonder once more what she might be up to.

It started at breakfast, when Josephine arrived earlier than Simon but at nearly the same time as her younger sisters and their governess.

Josephine said little until Rosalind brought up the idea of visiting the village.

"We must ask your brother for permission, dear," Mrs. Robinson said, hardly looking up from her plate. The woman had a motherly way about her, especially after she'd had her morning tea. "In your parents' absence, Lord Farleigh decides what is prudent."

"We cannot be in any danger here," Isabelle said, looking to Josephine and then Andrew for confirmation. "The people here are not like those in London. There is no reason for us to stay locked up in the castle."

"No one is locking you up, Isabelle." Josephine's lips twitched, then she pushed her food about on her plate, giving it more attention than her sister as she said, "But I do not think you ought to hope for such an outing so soon after arriving home. Simon may still be affected by what happened in London. If I were you, and I wanted to be certain of approval, I would wait until everyone has settled in at the castle before trying to leave it."

"That sounds rather sly of you." Andrew had already finished eating his breakfast and waited only for Simon before excusing himself. While he might not be under Simon's charge, he had accompanied his friend to be of use to him. Checking to ascertain whether he was needed first thing was the polite thing to do.

"Not sly," Josephine protested, laying her fork down without tasting anything. "Though I will say I have some experience in getting our parents to see things more favorably than they might if I made requests the moment they came into my head. I cannot see why Simon would be any different."

"You cannot mean to say that you manipulate your parents." Andrew had to scoff at that. He knew no two people so clever and level-headed as the Duke and Duchess of Montfort. "I imagine they allow you to think you have an influence on their decisions more than what it is in reality."

"Oh dear," Rosalind whispered into her spoon of fried potatoes.

Before Andrew could ask what distressed Rosalind, Josephine had squared her shoulders and narrowed her eyes at him. Rather as though she prepared herself for battle. Rosalind had perceived the pending argument before he had readied himself for it.

It was early yet for their usual volley of words, but Andrew folded his arms and grinned at Josephine in that way he knew she found most irritating. He canted his head to one side and let her see his amusement.

"I do not manipulate anyone. I merely wait until the most opportune moment to ask my questions or make my requests. I use sound judgement, nothing underhanded. I cannot believe you would imply such a thing about me, Sir Andrew."

"Lady Josephine." He threw her title back at her, drawing it out more than necessary. "The most opportune moment? You sound as though you view yourself as a strategist."

"Indeed, I certainly do. As my parents have raised me to embrace strategy and logic in my education, they would find no fault with it." She sounded almost haughty, and that one eyebrow arched up slowly. It was the way she ended arguments she thought she had won—that eyebrow.

Andrew wouldn't cede to her this time. "I would think a duke's daughter capable of both those things, though I doubt her parents would mean for her to practice such skills on them when she wants some new frippery, or to attend a soiree, or requires more pin money." He knew well enough that Josephine didn't exude the usual airs of spoiled nobility. No one in her family would stand for it, especially the duke. But she knew her place in Society well enough to take advantage of it from time to time.

He doubted she could help it. One born to such high privilege rarely knew what such a thing would mean to those watching her exercise it every day of her life.

"You make my capabilities sound incredibly trite, Sir

Andrew." She mirrored him, tilting her head at precisely the angle he held his own. "While I cannot imagine what you have against common sense, as that is all I would call my ability to wait until a situation favors my arguments or requests, I am quite aware that you rarely exercise it yourself."

It took a measure of control not to laugh aloud at her expert thrust. Especially when he heard Isabelle's mutter of, "Here we go again." The family was all too familiar with their battles of wit. Usually, everyone ignored them.

He meant to win this battle today, too. "You needn't concern yourself with my senses, any of them, or lack thereof. I manage perfectly well." He tapped the arm of his chair with one finger. "Though I should like to know an example of your *superior* skills. Tell me, my lady, can you think of a time when you have so neatly presented your requests, as you say, to your dear parents?"

A light pink hue tinted the apples of her cheeks. She glanced at her sisters. "It is not as though I performed a coup of some sort. As I said, it is only logic. Common sense. I never ask Papa for something I would like when he is in an unfavorable mood."

"You must explain to me with greater detail, or I am afraid I may never understand." Andrew leaned forward, toward her side of the table. "Surely you have at least one example you might share, for everyone's enlightenment?"

Before she could answer, Simon came into the room. He wore clothing for riding, which gave Andrew pause. He hadn't planned on either of them getting on the back of their horses again so soon.

"Do you know how much I enjoy beginning my day listening to the two of you argue?" he asked, his face a mask of disinterest. "Good morning, Mrs. Robinson. Isabelle. Rosalind." He looked from Andrew to Josephine. "Combatants."

"That isn't at all fair," Josephine chided. "We do not argue every morning."

Andrew caught the two younger sisters exchanging another

exasperated glance and had to chuckle. "Only most mornings," he admitted for them both.

"Dare I ask what it is this time?" Simon directed the question not at his friend or sister nearest him in age, but to Rosalind, the youngest at the table.

She settled her hands together upon the table. "Josephine has claimed she is an expert at getting what she wants from our parents by timing her approach to them. Andrew is demanding an example that she has yet to give."

"Is that all?" Simon nodded to a footman to bring him hot coffee. "A fairly mild topic for the two of you." He did not quite smile at Josephine, though Andrew thought his friend's eyes twinkled with amusement.

Good. Simon ought to laugh more. Even if it wasn't out loud. And at Andrew's expense. The duke's eldest took himself far too seriously sometimes.

With that, the subject of Josephine's abilities dropped, and Rosalind took up her cause for a trip to the village of Lambsthorpe.

"I want to look in on the shops and be sure our friends know we have returned," the young lady said, oblivious to her brother's frown. "We needn't purchase anything. I used all my pin money in London. But it would be lovely just to walk about the little village freely."

"It would serve you better to write letters to your friends, rather than hoping for a chance to run into them in the village." Simon looked to their governess. "Do you not agree, Mrs. Robinson? Letter writing is an essential skill for any lady, is it not?"

"It is indeed, my lord." The governess had the grace to sound thoughtful rather than disapproving of her charge's attempts to escape the castle. "Perhaps we might instead petition you to issue an invitation to the young ladies your sisters most wish to see."

Isabelle sighed, and Rosalind sunk somewhat in her seat with her bottom lip protruding. Of the duke's three daughters,

Josephine had always shown the most sense and decorum, even when she had been their age.

He remembered her at that age well, as she had been only a little younger than Isabelle when he had come to live with the family on a nearly permanent basis. At fourteen, nearly fifteen, she'd wasted no time in putting him in his place when he'd attempted to tease her.

Neither of them had stopped trying to get the better of the other since.

Which made it quite easy to keep their banter light, to make it his excuse for being near her and countering her every argument with one of his own, without anyone suspecting Andrew's perception of Josephine had changed. If he kept treating her as he had when he saw her as a child, no one would ever guess how much he had grown to admire the woman she had become.

When Josephine excused herself from the table without any attempt to bring up their argument again or start one afresh, Andrew watched her withdraw from the room with curiosity. She looked over her shoulder once, at Simon, and in a single unguarded second, Andrew saw a look upon her face she had worn rarely—an expression of guilt.

It reminded him of when he'd caught her in the corridor two evenings previous. Her gaze lowered to his, and her expression went blank, then she vanished through the doorway.

Curiosity piqued, Andrew looked to see if anyone else had noticed the odd behavior. Yet breakfast continued as normal—or as normal as it could without the ducal parents present—and no one said a word about Josephine.

If Andrew meant to discover what she was up to, he would have to go about it by himself. Perhaps not the best course of action, but certainly the most entertaining.

He hid his grin from the others as he considered spending yet more time in Josephine's company.

# CHAPTER 8

M isleading her family members as to her whereabouts wasn't something Josephine enjoyed, though she had become quite good at it since the previous summer. It was all a matter of timing and of leaving room for others to infer her whereabouts without actually confirming her plans.

After Josephine left her grandmother's favorite sitting room, implying she went to the nursery, Josephine instead took herself to her room to dress for a walk. If anyone saw her leave the castle, she would suggest that the gardens were quite lovely and the weather perfect.

Even if the clouds were looking a touch gray, it wasn't actually raining.

With a few careful turns in the garden, she would come out on the road that led to the castle at a distance far enough that no one would see her. The escape hardly counted as one, given the ease of her plan. Her sisters currently thought she was with their grandmother, who they would avoid before tea while they saw to their studies. Their grandmother thought Josephine had business in the schoolroom. She had hinted to one of the footmen tasked with the protection of the family that she had every intention of taking a nap.

When she slipped into the servants' staircase near the chapel, and then out the chapel doors to the lesser-used garden of topiaries, she did not see another soul.

Her plan went well. She was soon free of the gardens and upon the road to Lambsthorpe. After traveling down its length a short distance, she could take the shortcut she and her siblings frequently used to lessen her time in full view of anyone coming or going from Clairvoir.

The canopy of bright green leaves above made the path more shadowed than usual, and the spring growth of ferns, grasses, and hedge leaves created a living wall to block out the sound from surrounding fields. Bird calls sounded in the distance, but rarely from above. And while Josephine knew sheep and cattle dotted the fields on either side of her path, she did not hear them.

Dried leaves from the year before crunched under her boots. Occasionally, the wind made the leaves above ripple and shiver, sounding like they trembled beneath raindrops, though the clouds above had yet to break.

"A perfect spring day," Josephine said aloud, needing to hear a sound other than the quiet rustle of leaves. Had she ever made this walk on her own? No. Never. Always she had been with her sisters, or her brother, or at least her dearest Emma. How, at nearly twenty years of age, had she never been alone on their path before?

She had never taken the road by herself, either. Even on horseback, there had always been a guard or groom to accompany her on her rides or brief visits to friends nearby.

"I am perfectly capable of going about on my own," she murmured, looking through the trees at a stretch of green field, empty of livestock. The clouds above shifted, and the sky darkened enough that the path before her appeared less cheerful than before.

Her step faltered, then Josephine forced herself to laugh. The sound was rather lonely. "I know this path as well as the castle gardens. I have taken it a hundred times before. I am perfectly capable of walking to the village on my own." She adjusted the ribbons of her reticule, then patted the top of her bonnet, and stepped forward again with confidence—

The mad shriek of a pheasant burst from a bush beside her while the animal itself took off at a run across the track, startling Josephine so much that she screamed and moved backward. Her boot heel caught the hem of her skirt and tore, but she kept from falling by stumbling sideways into the trunk of a young tree. Her shoulder knocked into the unyielding bark, and Josephine had to bite her lip to keep from crying out again.

Glaring at the break in the undergrowth where the pheasant had disappeared, she thought several choice words about the horrible fowl. Never in her life had she undergone a fright such as that one.

"I hope the gamekeeper catches you," she called out to the bird. "And that Cook stuffs you with chestnuts and raisins, then serves you for dinner!"

The petty wish didn't make her feel any better. Her heart kept a frantic rhythm for several minutes after she resumed her walk. Another pheasant attack felt imminent.

It took ages to climb the last rise in the land, which would put her atop the hill overlooking Lambsthorpe, including its little church and the vicarage that stood nearby. When she saw the rise ahead, and she stepped out of the trees, a sense of relief washed over her that made her knees momentarily go weak. With her gaze trained upon the wildflowers waving atop the hill, she stepped out from beneath the cover of the trees.

"Ah. Here you are. I was beginning to wonder if you'd lost your way."

No. It could not be—

Josephine turned to the right at the same moment a large

golden-yellow horse snorted. Honey. Tied to a tree while her rider, the most disagreeable man in all of England, lay sprawled in the grass with an elbow propping him up. He grinned at her.

"How?" Josephine asked. The word stretched as it left her lips, her mind searching for any possible explanation for Andrew's appearance. No one had seen her—she'd been certain of it.

He waggled his eyebrows at her. "How, indeed. Life is full of mysteries, Josie."

She did not bother correcting his familiar use of her family's pet name. Not this time. Her irritation had yet to overtake her confusion. "No one saw me," she insisted, despite his presence offering evidence to the contrary.

"Two someones saw you." He sat up and brushed off his sleeves, then stood and stretched. Languidly. As though nothing in the world was amiss. "Simon and I had returned from our ride, and we came to the castle rise at nearly the same moment you stepped into the trees. The timing was most fortunate."

"If Simon saw me," she said, folding her arms over her midsection, "why did he not come after me? Why didn't either of you stop me?"

"Your brother had an important appointment with the land steward. You know how he is about his obligations in your father's absence." Andrew shrugged somewhat dismissively. "He asked me to fetch you home."

"He did not mean for you to come all the way to the village and lie in wait like some sort of wolf," she said, scowling at him. After the fright she had in the woods, and the uncertainty of walking a well-worn path alone for the first time in her life, coming upon Andrew was not a happy surprise. Not in the least.

Andrew's grin returned, larger than before and unrepentant. "Likely not, but this method was much more entertaining than stopping you earlier." He took a sauntering step toward her, and then another, amusement in his eyes and confidence in his posture. "How was your daring adventure, my lady? Did you come upon any bandits? Dragons? Perhaps a fairy in disguise?" He did not stop until he stood nearly toe-to-toe with her, his smile almost wicked.

Her heart picked up speed as it had after her fright. Indignation made her hands tremble—nothing else would make her react with such strength to Andrew's nearness. Nothing else would cause her cheeks to flush with warmth or the skin along her arms to prickle.

How dare he mock her?

"What is this?" His voice dropped low, to a teasing murmur. "Have I left you speechless? Wonder of wonders." He bent his head down, eyebrows lifted. "Shall I escort you back to the castle, now that the adventure is over?"

Josephine came to herself at last. "You may return to the castle without me," Josephine said, chin tipped so she might glare at him. Truly, it was quite inconvenient that he was taller than she. Perhaps he saw it as an advantage of some sort, to look down upon her. "I have no intention of allowing you to 'fetch me home.'"

Andrew's chuckle, low and soft, made her want to shiver where she stood. She hated how superior that single sound made him seem. "You haven't much choice in the matter. No one knew you were going out, nor granted you permission to wander about on your own. Come. I'll walk with you." He didn't move from where he stood, waiting for her to capitulate, no doubt.

"I have business to tend to in the village." Her gaze lowered from his twinkling eyes to his smirking lips. She stared at his mouth, positively annoyed by it. How dare he smirk at her? "I made my way here well enough, and I will return home the same. You needn't worry about me."

She stepped around him with a deliberate speed meant to look like confidence when, in reality, she wanted to get away quickly.

But Andrew had cursed-quick reflexes, and his hand nabbed her forearm. "Josie. You cannot wander around unchaperoned. It isn't proper for a young woman, especially one of your standing."

She tugged her arm away and narrowed her eyes at him. "I am the duke's daughter. I may come and go as I please, and *you*, a mere baronet, have no say in the matter."

He snorted. "Your attempt to use your rank is noted, but it is ridiculous. Even if you were serious, I am under orders from your brother, an earl and the duke's heir. And I cannot think your grandmother, or your parents, would approve of you casting off their rules."

She kept walking up the hill. "Go and tell my grandmother, then." She was bluffing, of course. If Grandmama found out what Josephine was up to, and why, she would berate her granddaughter for years to come.

Boots thumped the ground behind Josephine, quickly gaining on her. She expected Andrew to catch her arm again, and her heart rose into her throat. But he did not touch her. Only grumbled from behind. "What do you have to do that is so important it could not wait for your brother's escort? Or so secretive you must see to it alone?"

She stopped, now at the top of the hill, and looked back at him. Then her eyes went to his horse. "You mustn't leave Honey all alone out here. She is too fine a horse to be unprotected."

His jaw dropped a moment, then he looked back at the horse and up at her again. Incredulous. "You are worried about my unattended horse and not about yourself, as an unattended young lady?"

Josephine tightened her hands into fists, turned, and marched down the hill toward the road. She would visit the rector today, no matter Andrew's protests. She had done nothing wrong.

A moment later, she heard a horse coming down behind her and turned to see Andrew striding after her, leading his horse behind. "We should return to Clairvoir, Josie."

"I have things to do, *Andrew*." She kept walking, outpacing him. He stopped protesting and followed. Unwilling to leave her to herself. As she knew he would be.

Josephine bit her lip to keep from smiling. He might have surprised her, turning up at the end of her path as he had, but she had won the battle. This time.

ANDREW HAD NO INTENTION OF LETTING JOSEPHINE WIN. She might think she had the upper hand, leading him down the hill and into the village, but she was wrong. He would stay as close to her as necessary, and he would take her home in due course. Then he would let slip to her grandmother that Josephine had been to the village and let *that* teach Josephine for wasting his time.

Not that he had much else to do with it as a guest at the castle.

Planning his interception of the woman walking alone in the wood had been the high point of his day. The look on her face when he'd spoken, her surprise and dismay, had made sitting in the damp grass worthwhile. Somehow, he would come off the victor after following her about town on whatever errand she undertook.

They passed down the middle of town, with Josephine nodding to those who recognized her but not stopping for conversation. As a duke's daughter, it was up to her to approach someone. Rarely would anyone, even the wealthiest landowner's wife, presume to begin a conversation with a member of the duke's family.

Andrew nodded politely to those who looked his way, noting to himself who appeared censorious rather than curious. Most in the village knew that Andrew was treated like a member of the family. There could be no strong objection to his escort of Lady Josephine. Still. No use providing anyone with gossip.

When Josephine walked all the way to the church without stopping, Andrew's curiosity grew. The church, a medieval building as old as the village itself, was on the opposite end of the village from where they had entered it. And nearly the last building before the road led to open farmland.

What was Josephine trying to accomplish?

Finally, she stopped at a small iron gate in front of the vicarage.

Andrew peered at the unassuming little cottage. He had visited before, when Mr. Gooch was in residence. The vicar had invited Andrew and Simon to dinner.

Josephine opened the gate.

"You cannot mean you came all this way to visit Mr. Wood," Andrew blurted, catching the gate before she could close it between them. "That isn't at all appropriate, Josie."

She smiled prettily at him and batted her eyelashes innocently. "Seeking counsel from my spiritual leader is inappropriate?"

He opened his mouth and closed it again, uncertain for a moment. Then he shook his head. "You never sought out Mr. Gooch."

"How do you know?" she asked, her lips curling upward. "Do you spy on all my comings and goings? Why, Andrew. I am flattered you care so much."

A shift somewhere near his heart made him falter and grasp for a response, but she giggled and turned away. She went to the cottage door. Without him.

Andrew hastily tied up his horse at a ring protruding from the wall, then stepped through the gate. His long strides diminished the distance between him and Josephine in seconds, and he stood by her side by the time she raised her hand to use the knocker.

He beat her to grasping the iron ring. She blinked at him and smiled, tucking her hands behind her. Chiding her wouldn't result in any satisfaction, so he gave in and knocked upon the door. Then folded his arms across his chest and waited, shoulder-to-shoulder with Josephine. Not giving her an inch.

She hummed to herself, appearing perfectly content with the world and her place in it.

Then the door opened, and Mr. Wood himself stood there. Appearing somewhat befuddled. "Good afternoon. I apologize for the delay. There is no staff at present, you see, and—" He stopped, looking from Josephine to Andrew and back again.

"My lady. Sir Andrew. I did not expect to see either of you again so soon." He stepped back and gestured inside, but stopped short of inviting them in. Realizing, most likely, that two bachelors and an unmarried duke's daughter had no business closing themselves up in a house together. No matter how innocent the situation might be.

Josephine, always perfectly aware of Society's dictates, bestowed one of her warmest smiles on the rector. "Mr. Wood, I am glad you are at home. I wonder if I might have a moment of your time? There is a bench in the churchyard I thought I might show you. Mrs. Gooch has the loveliest little flower garden planted nearby, making it a perfect place for conversation."

Mr. Wood looked from Josephine to Andrew, but when Andrew said nothing, he addressed himself to the duke's daughter. "I am happy to speak with you, Lady Josephine. If you will let me get my hat?"

"Of course." She stepped back from the door and turned away to look across the road.

The rector sent another curious stare in Andrew's direction, then ducked back into the cottage. Andrew shook his head. "You are going to confuse the poor man, Josie. What could you possibly want from him?"

"When a young lady wishes to speak to her ecclesiastical steward, it is no affair of anyone else." Josephine peered over her shoulder at him. "No one asked you along, if you will recall."

Before Andrew could remind her that Simon had, in fact, asked Andrew to look after Josephine, Mr. Wood emerged with hat atop his head and gloves on his hands. He bore a somber expression again, too.

He looked up at Andrew. "Are you joining us, Sir Andrew?"

"Of course not," Josephine answered before Andrew said a word. "Though I am certain he will hover nearby." The glare she cut Andrew made him grin.

"Like an unwanted specter," he quipped, quite forgetting Mr. Wood's unfamiliarity with their ways.

"Oh." The clergyman looked between them with undisguised suspicion. "Very well then. Allow me, Lady Josephine." He offered her his arm. Josephine did not even look in Andrew's direction again as the rector led her down the path, through the gate, and to the churchyard and the aforementioned bench.

Andrew followed, pausing only long enough by his horse to check the security of the tied-off lead. This put a few steps between him and the couple walking arm-in-arm. Honey raised her head and snorted. "I quite agree. She is an odd one."

If Josephine heard, she gave no indication of it.

Andrew stopped at the stonewall that bordered the church-yard, leaning back against it and keeping an eye on Josephine as she settled on the bench. Though he found it impossible to fathom *why* she needed to speak to Mr. Wood, he had no reason to invade her privacy. Whether she spoke on a matter of theology, confession, or wished to ask the man's opinion on her bonnet, Andrew could grant her a moment's peace.

She wasn't the little girl he had met, all those years ago. She had been clever and sharp-tongued, and amusing to tease. But now... Josephine, a woman grown, was so much more. She was beautiful. Quick-witted. Intelligent. And thinking for even one moment that she would put herself in danger—it had made his temper flare, though that fire was fueled with worry for her safety.

The churchyard felt gloomier than usual. Likely because of the low-hanging clouds above them. The morning had taken on a gray cast shortly before Andrew and Simon had returned from their ride. As the rain had yet to break, they might get lucky and see none of it that day.

He focused once more on his errant quarry, settled happily on the bench with head upturned.

The rector remained standing, hands tucked behind his back. He wore an earnest expression as Josephine spoke, too quietly for Andrew to hear more than the tone she used. A soft, determined sort of tone.

He waited. And would wait as long as necessary to ensure she found her way safely home again.

# CHAPTER 9

W hile the sky overhead grew gloomier, Josephine asked Mr. Wood as many questions as she could think to without giving away the reason behind them. He was gentleman enough not to pry into her reasons for asking about his training, the life of a rector, or how he intended to become a vicar and what difference that would make in his role in the church. He also answered her questions about the vestry garments, confirming some of her knowledge while yet offering greater insight.

The interview lasted a quarter of an hour. All the while Josephine and Mr. Wood spoke, Andrew leaned against the stone wall. Arms crossed. Glancing about himself as though he hadn't anywhere or any way better to spend his time.

"Thank you for taking the time to answer my questions, Mr. Wood. You have assuaged my curiosity with such kindness." Josephine rose from the bench, and Mr. Wood was good enough to not look at his pocket watch. "If I think of anything else, might we speak again?"

"Of course. It is refreshing to find someone with such an interest in the work of a rector. I cannot think anyone has interviewed me so thoroughly before, not even when I took orders."

His smile, though tinged with amusement, remained perfectly polite. "I confess, Lady Josephine, when I opened the door to find you and Sir Andrew present, I thought my afternoon would take quite a different turn."

She glanced to where Andrew still waited for her, then back to the rector. "Oh? What did you expect would happen?"

His smile turned sheepish. "I have been told that when young couples turn up on a priest's doorstep without kin, they usually wish to discuss the possibility of marriage without parental permission."

Josephine could not stop her mouth from falling open in surprise, but she hastily closed it again and shook her head tightly. "Sir Andrew and me—the idea! You have not known us any measure of time, certainly, or you would see what an impossibility such a thing would be." She refrained from wrinkling her nose. Barely. "We scarcely tolerate one another."

"Truly?" Mr. Wood had the good grace to accept her pronouncement with an amused chuckle. He glanced at Sir Andrew. Then looked back at Josephine with raised eyebrows. "He is a fierce friend and protector. You must allow for that much."

"What makes you think such a thing, Mr. Wood?" How could anyone so misinterpret the irritation she and the baronet caused one another? A friend, indeed. He was Simon's friend. And *her* annoyance.

Josephine tried not to glance in Andrew's direction, but his relaxed stance stayed at the corner of her eye anyway. The walk home would trap them together soon enough.

Mr. Wood relaxed his posture. "Only the obvious, my lady. He has stood watch over us without question or complaint for the entirety of our interview."

"Oh." She relaxed. Mr. Wood thought Andrew worried after her. That was not so terrible a presumption on his part. "That is my brother's doing. Sir Andrew and Lord Farleigh are dear friends. My brother asked Sir Andrew to see me safely home this afternoon. That is all."

The rector's expression did not change, which made her wonder if his impression of Andrew remained the same. "Then I will allow him to see you returned to the castle safely, my lady. Thank you for your conversation. I hope my answers proved helpful to you."

"They have. Thank you once more." She curtsied, then turned to leave the churchyard, walking toward Andrew. He pushed himself away from the wall and fell into step beside her before she reached the arched exit to the road.

She did not say a word to him, though she waited at the lane for him to retrieve his horse from the vicarage. With Honey following behind, Andrew rejoined Josephine, and they walked together through the village on their way home to the castle.

They passed fewer people this time. Mr. Holton, the purveyor of ribbons and thread, hurried to gather his tall stand of ribbons. He took it indoors. Noting his anxious behavior, Josephine looked up at the sky.

Andrew followed her gaze. "I think it will hold until we get to the castle."

"Even if it does not, a little rain will hurt nothing." She checked the ribbon of her bonnet, finding it secure as ever beneath her chin. "Especially if we take the shortcut. There are plenty of trees overhead to block most of the rain."

"Honey cannot take the shortcut." Andrew gestured behind him to his large mare. "The path is too narrow and the trees too low for a horse of her size to pass through."

"Then I suppose the two of you will take the road." Josephine gave him her sweetest smile, batting her lashes at him. "And I will return home the way I came. Alone, via the shortcut."

"Josie." Andrew released a put-upon sigh. "I am not leaving you to walk home alone. You should never have come that way to begin with." They were through the village and coming down the last little hill before meeting the road that would wind through the wood and take them upward to the castle. Not a walk for one to make unless they were quite sure of their legs.

"You and my brother come and go as you please," she returned, keeping her voice airy and light. "I cannot see why it's so difficult for you to believe me capable—"

Andrew's hand caught hers, his gloved fingers firm, and he stopped Josephine where she stood. She turned to glare at him, though she did not give him the satisfaction of tugging her hand away. Which may have been a mistake on her part.

Because Andrew stepped closer, putting them merely a hand's breadth apart. He gave her a stern look. "I believe you are perfectly capable, my dear Josie."

For some odd reason, her throat closed up, making her throat go dry. He stood too near for politeness' sake. But then, when was Andrew ever polite to her? "Th-thank you."

He squeezed her hand at the same moment his lop-sided grin appeared. "Capable of getting yourself in trouble." He released her before she had the satisfaction of pulling away. He chuckled and kept walking.

Josephine hurried to catch up to him. But she kept to the opposite side of the road. She'd learned her lesson when it came to allowing him near. It addled her too much for her comfort. "Trouble? When have I ever found trouble without your involvement?"

"The Arcade comes to mind." He kept walking, wearing an infuriating and superior expression. "Or after the theater, when you became separated from your family and the guards."

"Again, you were with me both times. One could surmise those things were your fault."

"Really?" He looked across the lane at her. "What would you have done at the Arcade, had I not been there?"

"Sterling was with me. He kept me safe."

"Without confronting the troublemakers."

"That is not his job. He is only to keep the family from harm."

"And allow others to be disturbed, insulted, and possibly hurt."

He had a point, but Josephine could not let him know it. "That is not the point. The point is, I would have been safe."

"Because you had your guard. Where is Sterling now, Josephine?" He demanded of her, driving his point deeper. "At the castle. Unaware of the fact that you are far from its walls. Does anyone know where you went? When will they know you are missing if you do not return? Hours from now?"

A drop of water landed on the bridge of her nose. She wiped it away, irritated at the distraction.

"No one will know I have gone," she snapped, fuming. Why had Simon sent Andrew after her? Why not a guard? They wouldn't attempt to scold her. None of them would say a word to her. They would follow in silence.

Andrew had the terrible habit of telling her exactly what he thought. All the time. Whenever it pleased him. Even if she did not care what he had to say, or he only wished to tease her.

"What if you became lost?" he asked, stopping to bark the question at her. "Or turned your ankle on a tree root and could not walk unassisted? When would we know to come for you? How would anyone know where to find you?"

She jerked her gaze away from his, unsettled by his hard stare. Annoyed that he made a valid point in his argument. "Nothing happened."

"What if someone would have come upon you, walking all alone, Josie?" Andrew's voice dropped, his tone deep and concerned. "An enemy to your father, perhaps. A tenant who felt wronged. A poacher. Anyone with a black heart, for that matter, coming upon a defenseless woman wandering about without a chaperone or protector. What would you do if someone meant to hurt you?"

She bit her lip as cold shame washed through her. She knew better. Of course she did. But she had a purpose in going alone.

Everything to do with her book, her writing, she had done alone. It belonged to her and no one else. The words on the page, the research, the hours spent day-dreaming in the tower, even the puzzling rejection letter, they were all hers.

Setting out on her own had seemed right at the time. But now, beneath the weight of Andrew's words, she recognized the truth of what she had done. She had behaved selfishly. So much so that Josephine knew how disappointed her parents would be if they ever found out.

And she had accomplished her goal, even with Andrew attending her. A guard wouldn't have questioned her, either. She would have stayed safe, as her parents wished, and still accomplished her purpose.

Her jaw quivered. But she would not cry. Not in front of Andrew. Never would she give him that satisfaction. Except her chest tightened uncomfortably. Her eyes grew hot. Raindrops pattered along the back of her neck, between her bonnet and gown.

How had she acted so exceptionally foolish? And why did Andrew have to be the person to point it out to her?

Sensing his words had at last made the duke's eldest daughter think on more than her own designs, Andrew drew closer to her. He kept one hand gripped tightly on Honey's lead. The other he used to touch Josephine's cheek, tilting her chin up, so she had to face him.

A few tears had escaped her eyes. Whether they were born of frustration or hurt, he did not know. But despite all their years of antagonizing one another, he had no wish to see her cry. Especially now, when they were not the frustrated tears of a child caught in a wrong act. These were the tears of a woman, coming to terms with her place in the world and the danger around her.

He kept his tone soft when he spoke again, but they bore no less weight than before. "What would your family do, your father and mother, if someone hurt you?" What would *he* do if something awful befell her?

Josephine sniffled. "You are right. Of course." Did it pain her so much to say those words aloud? He nearly asked. But with her admittance, he had much rather have peace between them.

So instead of grinning and insisting she repeat those rare words, Andrew brushed her cheek with his thumb. "If you need to sneak off again, tell me. I would rather play your shadow and keep your secrets than see harm come to you." The sincerity with which he said those words momentarily surprised him.

Keep her secrets? Where had that promise come from?

The way her dark blue eyes, shining with tears, brightened at the suggestion, caused a knot within his chest to twist almost painfully. But her slow smile kept him from regretting his words. "Do you believe I have many secrets, Sir Andrew?"

They stood close. So close he could count the dark lashes framing her beautiful eyes one by one, if he wished. The tilt of her lips conveyed both humor and a certain vulnerability—unless he imagined it.

He had to be imagining it. When had he ever seen Josephine vulnerable? The chit had more power in her little finger than all other women of his acquaintance.

But that was precisely the problem, wasn't it? A duke's daughter wasn't brought up to fear much of anything.

What had they been speaking of? Andrew swallowed, but uncertainty closed his throat and arrested his tongue. The world went still around them, the only sound the rush of his pulse in his ears, her soft breath, and the patter of rain upon the leaves. Her smile melted away into a frown of puzzlement.

They had stood still for too long.

A drop struck his wrist, another fell upon her nose, and quite suddenly, they were in the deluge. A cold, swift fall of rain broke through the fog of his thoughts. Andrew drew back from Josephine at the same moment he looked up at the ominous gray clouds.

"We have run out of luck, it would seem," he grumbled. Honey knickered as though in agreement, though the horse could not possibly understand the sudden confusion of his thoughts. Why was he so disappointed his interlude with Josephine must end?

He would much rather be irritated she kept them out long enough to be caught in the spring rain.

Josephine held her arms out. "A fine fettle we're in now, sir." She looked from his horse up the hill. "We will be wet to the bone before we make it back to the castle." Her tone implied she held him responsible for their circumstance.

"If you would have returned home when I asked—"

She cut him, scoffing. "Asked? You know very well you *commanded* I return."

"I wouldn't dare command you, Josie. We both know you outrank me." He flashed her a grin he knew she would find irritating, and given the way her eyes narrowed at him, he was precisely right. "I still hold this is your fault, but I will be gentlemen enough to find a solution."

"Before my bonnet is entirely ruined, if you please." She cocked one eyebrow up at him, and he chuckled.

Considering the way the path wound around the hill, with canopies of leaves not entirely covering it, they were going to get wet. How long they remained that way was the only thing within his control.

"There is nothing for it, Josie. If we ride double on Honey, we will make better time than walking. That will get you out of this rain before you catch cold."

Her lips turned down with dismay. "Ride double? I have never—"

"Well, you are about to." He mounted as easily as he drew

breath, then looked down at her and held out his hand. "Come along. It will be easier if you do not give it much thought."

"Is that your philosophy for life or merely your horsemanship?" she asked, the words tart and disapproving.

"We can stand here in the rain and argue, or we can bear each other's company for the brief time it takes to ride up this hill. Either way, we will not have a dry stitch of clothing before we are home. How long you remain in your wet dress is up to you."

Her mouth fell open. "My clothing, wet or dry, is none of your concern."

Andrew groaned and looked up to the sky, wondering why his friend couldn't have a more sensible sister. "Josie, as entertaining as this is, please get on the horse."

"Riding double isn't good for Honey," she said, sounding somewhat less reluctant than before.

Though she was right, of course, there would be little danger to the animal given the short distance required for the mare to travel. "Just this once will not harm her. I promise."

She huffed. "I suppose this is the best option." She approached but did not take his hand. "I cannot ride sideways behind you. I will certainly fall off as we go uphill."

"Ride astride, then."

The scandalizing suggestion was worth seeing her expression. Her eyes widened and her cheeks turned pink. "Don't be ridiculous," she half-stammered, half-gasped.

He didn't laugh. Much. And he stopped when her frown appeared, complete with that single eyebrow raising with disapproval.

"Never fear. I know you are far too prim and proper to consider such a thing." Andrew shifted as far back as his saddle allowed, which was barely an inch. "Come along, Lady Josephine. You may ride in front of me, and I will ensure you do not fall into the mud."

All the while, the rain continued to fall. Soaking them slowly, but completely. The scandal of riding double on Honey was unlikely to be noted, given that most would keep indoors in the wet spring weather. They had only to make it up the hill, where no one else had reason to travel.

Josephine came to the same conclusion he did, apparently. She took his hand, and together their efforts saw her seated in the saddle in front of him. If not comfortably, at least efficiently.

Andrew's left arm went around her back to grasp the reins, his right sleeve brushed her abdomen. He nudged Honey forward, and the three of them started up the hill in relative silence. Josephine held herself stiffly at first, but then her right shoulder leaned into him.

"If you're cold," Andrew said as he noted the thin material of her dress, "you can lean in a little closer."

That made her turn to marble. "Are you suggesting I cuddle you for warmth? Does that sort of thing work with your conquests?"

"Conquests?" He chuckled. "I cannot say I have had many of those. Or any at all, if I am honest. Who put that idea into your head?" Did she think about his romantic life? How strange. He had wondered once or twice about hers over the course of the Season, but she'd never indicated she thought about the noblemen surrounding her, vying for attention. And he'd ignored them. Or made a sport of pointing out their oddities to her in the evenings, after a ball or social visit.

Quite suddenly, he thought on her visit that morning with Mr. Wood.

It seemed odd for Josephine to seek out the new rector. Unless she meant to size him up for something. Surely, no religious concern could send her out on her strange errand and still leave her in a pleasant mood. Pleasant for Josephine, anyway.

"No one suggested you have conquests." She shrugged, the shoulder touching him rising and falling against his chest. "I made an assumption."

"An unwise habit," he murmured, keeping his gaze on the road ahead of them. Ignoring the warmth that grew everywhere they touched. Her shoulder to his chest. The back of her knee to the front of his. His arm along her lower back.

Perhaps *failing* to ignore those small connecting places was a better description of his state of mind.

"You aren't much of a flirt, are you?" she asked, her voice quiet. "I cannot recall seeing you flirt with anyone."

A warning bell rang within his head. "I flirt." Sometimes. When he met a woman intelligent enough to spar with him. It was only that Josephine was his favorite verbal-fencing partner. Not that he flirted with her. Of course that description wouldn't fit their interactions.

That wasn't a productive path for his thoughts to travel. He tried to distract himself with something else.

Had Josephine always been so small? Seated as she was between his arms, he wondered why he had never realized how much they differed in size. Josephine was tall for a woman, but her entire family was somewhat above average in height. And he wasn't a small man himself. But they had never been this close, where he could note the dainty structure of her wrists and hands, the dip of her waist, the elegant curve of her neck....

"This is terribly awkward." Josephine's statement pulled him out of his spiraling thoughts. Spiraling to what, he did not know, nor did he think it a good idea to find out.

It seemed her thoughts had not run as wild as his own. Their unusual proximity hadn't disturbed her beyond physical discomfort.

As the gentleman, it fell to him to make things better. Even if it was her fault they were in the position in the first place. He cleared his throat. "It would be less awkward if we had a conversation."

"I doubt it," Josephine muttered as she leaned a little more into him. Only because—he told himself—of the steep road. "Sir Andrew?"

Ah, they had gone back to proper address, had they? Perhaps that was wise, given their circumstances. "Lady Josephine."

"How long do you intend to stay at the castle?"

He considered the question a moment before answering honestly. "I hadn't given it much thought. Simon asked if I would accompany him, and I said yes. I suppose until your parents return from London. Then I will see to my interests in Bytham."

His family's ancestral home, old and outdated as it was, needed little of his attention. The rundown building could hardly even be called a castle when compared to places like Clairvoir. His land steward saw to the tenants and farms reasonably well. There wasn't much for Andrew, as a bachelor, to do in the community.

Josephine cleared her throat. "I suppose you mean to make a nuisance of yourself, where I am concerned, during the entirety of your stay?"

"There you are, assuming things again."

"So you do not mean to act the part of my shadow?" Archness colored her voice, but maybe a hint of amusement, too.

"If it ceases to be diverting, I suppose."

She laughed. "You are most irritating, Sir Andrew."

He smiled to himself, not taking the jibe to heart.

The horse took an odd step, and Andrew looked down reflexively—causing a large drop of water to fall from the brim of his hat onto the exposed skin between Josephine's bonnet and coat collar. She gasped and jerked forward, making Honey shift and sidestep.

Andrew tightened his arms around Josephine to keep them both balanced on the horse, then he soothed the mare, speaking in a low voice. "Calm yourself, Honey. Step lightly. Everything is as it should be."

The horse's ears flicked back, listening to him, then forward again as she tossed her golden head. She resumed a steady gait, and a few moments after that, Josephine tipped her head up. She met his gaze, her blue eyes dark beneath the brim of her bonnet.

"Andrew?" The hushed way in which she spoke his name made that knot in his chest tighten again. Then, oddly, it uncoiled as he noted the worry in her eyes, the curve of her cheek, and the slight part to her lips. Soft, pink lips. Entirely kissable. Even when they curved into an uncertain frown. "You needn't keep hold of me so tightly."

"Oh." He immediately relaxed his arms and forced himself to look straight ahead. "My apologies." Heat crept up the back of his neck, hidden by his cravat, collar, and coat. He'd never been so grateful for the fashion of high collars in his life, especially as Josephine continued to peer up at him. Finally, she faced forward again, her bonnet shielding her from the gently falling rain and his gaze.

Had he really thought her kissable?

That one errant thought was a betrayal to Simon's trust. To the duke's! It wasn't his place to think about kissing Josephine. No matter the state of her lips or the delicate scent of her hair. What did it smell like? Something soft and feminine. Flowery. Entirely suitable to Josephine.

Andrew shook his head, mentally taking himself in hand.

The rain had addled his thoughts. Obviously.

But they could not arrive at the castle too soon for his liking. He needed to dry off. Then dunk his head in cold water to clear his muddied thoughts.

# CHAPTER 10

"Josephine? Is there something amiss between you and Sir Andrew?"

The question, voiced by her youngest sister in the gardens, caused all other thoughts in Josephine's mind to collapse like an ill-stacked stone wall. She dropped the stick of charcoal in her hand, and it landed on the apron she wore for their activity.

The governess, Mrs. Robinson, had invited Josephine to join her sisters in the gardens for an afternoon of sketching. Not for an inquiry.

"Why would you ask?" Josephine picked up her charcoal, not even glancing at Rosalind. "We are our usual selves to one another. He is unpleasant and tiresome. I am the very picture of patience and tolerance."

Isabelle snorted.

"Young ladies do not snort, dear," the governess said from behind her book. She sat on a bench nearby, where she could give direction without standing over them.

"Yes, Mrs. Robinson." Isabelle lowered her sketchbook. "Now that I think on it, you two have behaved rather strangely of late."

A week had passed since the ride home in the rain. Seven days in which Josephine had spent every moment in Andrew's presence feeling pensive about what he might reveal of their time together. Then oddly disappointed when he made no mention of it to her or anyone else in the household. Simon had not asked or said a word about sending Andrew to fetch her.

Which made her wonder all the more what Andrew had said to her brother about her walking into the woods unaccompanied.

"There is less bickering than usual." Rosalind shaded around her sketch of a fountain with a heavy hand. Sketching wasn't her strong suit, but she had a gift with music that made the whole family unreasonably proud.

Would they feel the same about Josephine's gift with words? Or her attempt to foster such a gift, she supposed. She had read through her entire manuscript again and was no closer to understanding what she had done wrong. Alternatively, she sometimes thought she had done nothing right, either.

If only Emma hadn't fallen in love with her Sicilian count, then Josephine would have someone to talk to.

Isabelle tapped at her chin, leaving a small smear of gray on her skin. "Do you think Sir Andrew considers himself a brother to us? I have often wondered, since he is so much older and forever with Simon."

"He likely does." Rosalind closed her sketchbook, finished for the day even if Mrs. Robinson intended for them to be at work longer. She hadn't much patience for things she was not already proficient in. "He has watched all of us grow up. Does it matter? He is so old."

"Mr. Gardiner is even older, but you thought him attractive. We both did."

"It was entertaining to watch him work," Rosalind conceded. "But his obsession with insects made him less attractive."

"Miss Sharpe didn't think so," Mrs. Robinson said from her place behind them on the bench, turning another page of her book. "Which is why she is Mrs. Gardiner now and it is up to me to tell you both that tea is in a quarter of an hour."

Josephine hid her smile and concentrated on her work. Her friend, and her sisters' former governess, Alice Sharpe, had fallen in love the summer before. She had come to the castle for employment and left as a bride. Shortly after, Emma Arlen had fallen in love with the ambassador, and left Josephine behind.

Now here she sketched in the gardens with her sisters, while her father and mother remained in London. And all she could think about was her failed manuscript and whether or not Andrew would really keep her secret.

He had said he would. And he had spoken with such fervency that she had believed him. At the time.

What a strange day that had been. Despite her determination to do otherwise, Josephine had caught herself remembering their rain-soaked ride up the hill. How strange it had been, to trust her well-being so fully to a man who had teased her to fits for half her life.

Though Andrew had acted with great maturity of late. And protectiveness, if she examined his behavior closely. At the Arcade, in front of the theater, and during their ride in the rain.

"Time to clean up," Mrs. Robinson announced before Josephine had muddled her way through any more thoughts. "Your grandmother will not want even a smudge of charcoal on your fingers when you take tea with her. Or on your chin, Isabelle. Rosalind, do help your sister."

Josephine quietly packed away her drawing things in her basket. Together, the four women walked through the gardens and into the castle. Her younger sisters chatted amiably with their governess, and Josephine lagged behind after they passed through the castle doors.

As she drifted up the staircase to the family wing, Josephine frowned to herself. When had Andrew grown so attentive toward her? And how had he managed to do so without her noticing?

There had been that moment the week before, when she had startled the horse. The sensation of Andrew's arms coming around her to hold her steady, to protect her from what would have been a nasty fall, had left Josephine quite forgetful of all their old arguments. Everything had faded away, even the momentary danger, as she'd realized Andrew would protect her no matter the circumstance.

The thought had proven both enlightening and disturbing.

Tea with her grandmother and sisters proved a welcome distraction for Josephine. Their grandmother had received a letter from the duke, which she read aloud to them, reassuring the family that the duke and duchess were well. There had been no new disturbances in London, though there were reports from other counties of political disquiet.

Grandmama tucked the letter away with a sniff. "There will always be those who are discontented with their place in the world."

Josephine bit her tongue. She knew her father's side of that argument quite well. He would say, *"No one can be content, let alone happy, when their concerns are unheard and their needs unmet."*

Though her father belonged to the conservative political party, he often crossed political lines in his pursuit of justice and hope for those in need of mercy.

Not long after that conversation, Josephine walked down the corridor into the family wing and passed by her room. No one had need of her, at present, which left her free to go up to the tower. As she slipped into the closet which hid the secret door, she considered her manuscript anew.

This time, she wondered what her father would make of her story. Would he be impressed with a clergyman who did little besides flirt with an orphaned maiden? Would the virtues of the heroine make her someone worth admiration, or was her inaction at pivotal moments in the story too weak?

Lost in thought, she ascended the tightly-wound spiral stair-case to the small room at the top of the tower. She did not realize until moments later that the click she heard when she cracked open one of the narrow stained-glass windows came from the bottom of the tower rather than outside its walls.

ANDREW HAD ONLY MEANT TO RETRIEVE A BOOK FROM HIS room. The innocent enough errand brought him into the corridor of the family wing an instant before Josephine opened a door he knew belonged to a closet of cleaning supplies.

He knew where several such closets were, given that he had no wish to make an enemy of the family's housekeeper by leaving the worst of his messes for a maid to discover. Ducking into closets to avoid certain guests or members of the family at inopportune moments also accounted for some of his knowledge.

When Josephine shut the door of the closet with her on the inside, he froze mid-step.

Was she hiding from him? No, she hadn't had time to see him. He'd barely glimpsed her profile before she'd vanished.

He took the last few steps to his door, then lingered a moment with his hand suspended above the handle. Josephine didn't emerge from the closet. Interesting.

He waited another moment, then shrugged and walked down to the concealed door. Only someone looking carefully for such a thing would recognize the closet for what it was. It blended almost seamlessly with the walls on either side of it, complete with a decorative swirl of wood at its top. But there was the slightest gap between the bottom of the door and the floor. A touch at waist-level meant finding a cleverly hidden handle. A quick tug, and he had the door open to reveal—

Cleaning supplies. Folded cloths. Buckets. Brooms. Featherdusters. An apron suspended on a hook. And absolutely no sign of the duke's eldest daughter.

Andrew stared hard at the smallish pantry. Then he stepped inside and closed the door behind him. Leaving him in darkness.

He stood perfectly still, listening. Sensing the air. Letting his eyes adjust to the dim, thin strip of light streaming through the narrow opening at the bottom of the door.

As a family friend who may as well be family, he knew of more than one secret passage in the castle. He wasn't to use them except in an emergency, like the rest of the family.

But he hadn't guessed there might be such a passage here. Though it made sense enough, so near the bedrooms of the duke's heirs. He stepped further into the darkness and put his hands out on either side of him. Testing the walls. Gently nudging hooks.

At the back of the closet, his finger found a narrow split in the wall that may have been nothing more than the uneven meeting of two boards. But he knew better.

For one brief instant, he considered leaving Josephine alone. He could walk out of the closet, close the door behind him, and pretend he hadn't seen a thing.

Except... He searched his mind for a credible reason to go after her. She was within the castle walls. That meant she was safe. Obviously, she wished for privacy, slipping away alone as she had. Josephine had spent most of her time alone of late. He had sensed on more than one occasion she missed Emma. Was that reason enough to follow her? Suspecting loneliness didn't mean it would please her to see him.

And that thought stung more than he thought it would.

Except what if she meant to do something foolish again, such as she had when she visited the rector without an escort?

With a gentle press in the right place, he opened the door in near silence, and soft blue light came through the doorway. He stepped through, careful to close it behind him, and looked up.

The winding staircase went both directions, descending into shadow and rising into light.

His feet took him silently upward, his intuition pointed him to Josephine. His mind turned about his mental map of the castle and he knew precisely where they were. The false tower.

He made not a sound, but he could hear the soft sound of Josephine's humming above him.

Then he turned the final step, bringing his eyes level with the landing—the only floor in the tower, shining in blues, golds, and lavender light that filtered through the stained glass in the faux arrow-slits meant for decoration rather than any practical purpose.

Until that moment, he had thought only two towers in the castle had any way to enter them. One was the clock tower, which served as a rookery for the duke's hunting birds. The other was in the center of the castle, where the duke's flag flew when he was in residence. The family used it mostly for storage.

But here he found Josephine, her back to him, as she leaned toward an open window, her head tilted to rest against the arched stone.

The room couldn't be more than eight feet in diameter. Worn rugs covered the floor. Cushions lay piled in the center, against the stone column rising from the staircase. Various other objects were scattered around the room, but he had no chance to inspect anything else.

Josephine ceased humming. Slowly, as though reluctant to discover what had disturbed her, and with rigid posture, she turned.

He took another step up, revealing head and shoulders to her. Then he took another step. He offered what he hoped she'd see as a non-threatening smile as he rose, step after slow step, until he was only one away from the landing. He leaned his shoulder against the stone column.

Josephine's hands opened and closed into fists at her side, over and over, and her face remained a mask of uncertainty.

"Andrew." Her eyes darted to the side where several books and a traveling desk were stacked atop one another. "What are you doing here?"

"I came to ask you that very thing." He hesitated. If he took that last step into territory she had clearly made her own, her calm facade would most likely explode in fury or indignation. Or something with a measure of both. He hovered as he would at any doorway when uncertain of his welcome. "I did not know there was a room here."

"I don't think anyone does." Josephine spoke with a tightness in her voice he hadn't heard before. "It isn't much of a room."

He looked about again, his eyes lingering on the glass. "Why are you up here all alone?"

She took a step forward. "I had rather not say."

Andrew raised his eyebrows. "Ah. Well then." He pushed away from the stone and tugged at his coat sleeves as though to straighten them. He had one last card to play. "Perhaps I will put that question to Simon. He might find your whereabouts of interest."

"Andrew, no." She rushed forward, coming to within a foot of him. "Please. Don't say anything to Simon. Or anyone else." She clasped her hands in front of her. "I have kept it to myself for so long. I have no wish to explain myself, or to have the tower invaded by anyone else." Her deep blue eyes pled with him so earnestly, he nearly felt sorry for threatening to speak to Simon.

Still. "No one else knows about you being up here?"

"Emma did." Josephine turned away from him, worrying her bottom lip between her teeth. "But only Emma."

Although the two ladies had always been thick as thieves, Emma had always had a practical mind beneath her playful nature. "What did my cousin think of your reason for being up here?"

"She understood. I think."

"And you do not think me capable of the same?" he asked, feigning insult.

"It isn't as though I have ever taken you into my confidence before." She paced away, murmuring, "Until lately."

"If you are referring to the visit we paid to the rector, I hope I have proven myself trustworthy in that regard."

She nodded. "You have. And I thank you for it. But this is... different." Her voice grew softer on the last word, and she lowered her gaze to the carpet.

Andrew rubbed the back of his neck as he studied the top of her dark hair, all swirls of deep brown and green ribbon. How could he convince her that he would keep her secret? What would it take to gain her confidence?

And why did it matter to him so much?

"Where did the carpets come from?" he asked, surprising her enough that Josephine lifted her gaze to his again. She lifted one eyebrow. That familiar arch look gave him permission to lean closer, drawing his brows together. "I cannot imagine you dragged them up here all on your own, but if no one knows of this room—"

"I brought them up. I borrowed them." She brushed at her gown. "They were from the old castle, left in closets here and there."

"No one caught you or thought to wonder why the duke's eldest daughter dragged old carpets around the castle?"

"I am quite good at being secretive." Her lips turned up in a wry—though brief—smile. "Until of late."

He chuckled. "I shouldn't be surprised. You are a determined woman when you put your mind to something." He let his words sink in, the compliment sincerely meant, and waited for her to fill the silence.

She pulled in a deep breath, looked down the steps behind him as though to be certain no one else waited to discover her, and then met his gaze with a steady one of her own. "Will you promise not to speak of this to anyone else?"

"Josie." He spoke the shortened, familiar form of her name with a gentle smile. "If you aren't doing anything dangerous," he said, "I have no reason to share your secret with anyone."

Her lips curled upward. "It is Josephine to you, Andrew."

"Not Lady Josephine?" he asked, his heart skipping a beat when he noted the tilt of her head. She had assessed him. And he had not been found wanting.

"Not if we are to share a secret, I suppose." She waved a hand between them dismissively. "And we have known each other since I was a child." She stepped back one step, then two. "Come in. The view from the window is lovely—and if you are to know my secret, I need to show you something."

When Emma had first come up to Josephine's tower, she had felt a thrill of excitement and hope. When Andrew took the last step inside, she marked a distinct difference in her feelings. Her heart pounded harder, and her cheeks grew warm. Her stomach twisted, though not unpleasantly, and she very much wanted to run and hide.

But there was no place to go. They were both in the tower. Alone. The room shrinking around them with each passing second.

Andrew walked by her to go to the window, and he looked out at the view as she had suggested. Saying nothing. Waiting for her to get her bearings, most likely. It was quite gentlemanly of him, even if he had threatened to expose her secret to her brother mere minutes before. As Simon's friend, she supposed Andrew owed her brother more loyalty.

Yet Andrew had already proven himself by not mentioning her trip to the village to anyone.

Josephine went to her pile of cushions and sat, as delicately as one could sit on the ground. She checked that her skirts covered all they should. Once she had organized her skirts and thoughts, she studied Andrew.

He stood in profile, peering out the window she had left slightly ajar. His light-brown hair looked gold, thanks to the yellow stained glass behind him. He made the room feel tiny, even though he wasn't a giant of a man. Not like her father. His head almost brushed the ceiling.

"Why did you follow me?" she asked. "That first night we returned to the castle, and now."

Andrew glanced her direction and shrugged. "I promised your father I would help Simon look after everyone. Your sneaking about seemed strange. I have never known you to be secretive, in all my years as a friend to the family. I thought you might need looking after."

"Is that why you followed me into the Burlington Arcade, too?" Josephine tucked her hands in her lap.

"Not at all." His teeth flashed as he smiled, then he lowered himself to the ground on his side of the circular room. Keeping a civil distance between them. "At the Arcade, I had every intention of disrupting your outing in as tedious a way as possible. For my own amusement."

A laugh escaped her. "You are ridiculous."

"I have never denied it."

Josephine smiled, and a cord around her heart loosened. She had been so lonely without Emma, and then separated from her parents, sent to the country while most of her peers remained in London. There had been no one to talk to. Not even Simon, busy as he had made himself with running the castle.

Perhaps Andrew sensed her need for a friend, and for once, he had chosen to sympathize with her rather than antagonize her. Though she could not know his reasoning, she allowed herself to be grateful. Just this once.

"What do you do up here, Josephine?" Andrew stretched one leg out and kept the other bent, putting his elbow on his knee and letting his posture relax. "Sit and daydream?"

"No. Well. Not entirely." She glanced again at the little traveling desk, and the books she had stacked on top of it. "I suppose you could call part of it daydreaming. Mostly, I write."

After a stretch of contemplative silence, he repeated back to her, "You write?"

"Yes." She tried not to fidget. Here it came. The moment she revealed a part of herself to him that only Emma, her dearest friend, had known about. Dare she trust Andrew? It wasn't too late. She could tell him—

"Writing letters? Or in your journal?"

Either of those would be the perfect excuse, the easiest way to cover the truth. Andrew waited with a patient expression, a near-smile, and eyes full of amusement.

Once he knew the truth, he would have power over her. Power and the ability to tease and torment her about something she held dear to her heart.

What on earth was she thinking? Why hadn't she dismissed him at once? Dared him to tell Simon? Shoved him down the stairs?

The thought of doing violence to any creature made her shudder. No. She had come this far. She might as well be honest. What was the worst thing that could happen?

She swallowed. "No. Neither of those things." She wrapped her arms around her midsection and closed her eyes. It would be easier if she did not see his expression right away. She'd rather not tell him at all. But he'd promised to keep her secret, so long as she wasn't hurting anyone. Authoring a book wasn't doing any harm.

He would keep her secret. Then, perhaps, he would leave her alone.

"I wrote a novel." She kept her eyes closed for the space of three breaths, and the surrounding air hung stiffly despite the open window. The silence stretched, longer and longer. Finally, she could stand it no longer. Still not looking at him, she spoke. Her words came out in a weak whisper. "Have you nothing to say?"

He must wish to torment her. Perhaps he could not think on where to begin.

"What sort of novel?" he asked, voice calm, tone curious and nothing more.

Josephine cracked one eye open to peer at him, disbelieving the simplicity of his question. To her everlasting surprise, he fixed his gaze upon her with stoicism rather than amusement or disbelief.

"Nothing ridiculous," she said, her words suddenly tripping one after another from her mouth. The need to justify herself, coupled with the relief of telling someone at long last, made for a strong combination. "It isn't a gothic novel, or anything to do with me, really. I wrote about a gentleman's poor daughter removing to a new community after her father's death, and how she must live with a spinster aunt. She has to find happiness despite her circumstances. The vicar helps her see others around her, and their plights, so she might learn compassion. Then she falls in love with the vicar, of course, and—" She cut herself off when she noticed how high Andrew's eyebrows had risen.

Josephine bit her tongue. Why had she mentioned the romance?

Andrew considered her quietly, his expression frozen. Then, somewhat cautiously, he said, "Does anyone else know?"

Squirming wasn't an option for a duke's daughter, but Josephine nearly performed the action anyway. She absolutely could not tell him the manuscript had already faced the worst sort of rejection—from a publisher. "Emma knew. Well. She knew I was writing *something*, but she doesn't know I've completed it. Or what it's about. Though she promised to read it."

Tilted his head back to rest it against the stone behind him,

Andrew narrowed his eyes at Josephine. He could not know what she left out of her explanation. As intelligent as he was—a thing she admitted reluctantly—he couldn't guess at her defeat.

"I am not surprised she supported your efforts. My cousin is the most dedicated reader I know." He looked at the stack of books and the writing desk. "It's in the box, isn't it? That is what you were trying to sneak up here. That night I caught you in the corridor."

Her hands twitched with the need to snatch everything up, to tuck it away from his sight. But she laced them together instead. Keeping them in her lap. Prim. Proper. Ladylike. "Yes."

"Ah." His lips twitched, and a gleam she knew all too well came into his eye. He opened his mouth, but before he could say anything, Josephine gave him what she hoped he'd see as a fierce and determined glare.

"You absolutely cannot tease me about this, Andrew. This is important to me. I have taken you into my trust, without much choice I might add, and if you attempt to use this against me for your own amusement, I promise on all that I love that I will *never* forgive you." She kept her gaze steady, not looking from his eyes, not drawing breath until she knew the truth of her words had sunk into her soul.

The gleam dimmed. His eyebrows raised slowly. "Very well. You have my word, as a gentleman, I will not tease you about this. Since it means so much to you."

"Good." She stood and brushed imaginary dust from her gown. "Now, if you will please be on your way. I have work to do, and you are decidedly underfoot."

He rose, though she thought she sensed some reluctance on his part. "Very well. If you find me so distracting to your purpose, I suppose I can be off."

"I do not find you a distraction."

"It sounds as though you do, since my being here hampers you so."

She pursed her lips and pointed to the stairs. "Out."

He chuckled and bowed with an extravagant wave of his hand. "Very well, my lady."

She huffed and put her hands on her hips. "Why do you do that? You know I detest such genuflecting." She already had to put up with dramatic gestures from acquaintances who thought one in her position would revel in such spectacles, meant to flatter a duke's daughter.

His grin turned impudent. "I suppose I owe you a secret, since I have one of yours." He stepped closer, confidence in his posture. Her throat closed, just as he leaned down to whisper in her ear. "It is precisely because you dislike it, my lady, that I tease you so." His low chuckle caused a flutter in her stomach. He was gone again before she could guess at why his nearness had caused that odd sensation.

Then he went to the top of the steps and looked over his shoulder at her, his eyes bright and expression merry. "Watching you color up and grow flustered is one of my favorite amusements when I visit the castle." Then he had the audacity to wink at her before disappearing down the steps.

Josephine growled in frustration. How dare he? She snatched up one of her cushions, ran to the top of the steps, and threw it after him, grazing his shoulder as he turned out of sight.

Her ill-aimed volley only made him laugh, and she felt the color he spoke of rising hotly into her cheeks.

Rather than stop to puzzle out why Andrew never failed to get a reaction from her when she could so easily wear her ladylike mask for everyone else, Josephine went to her desk and pulled out a blank sheet of paper and a pencil.

One ought never to annoy a writer, for who else could get their revenge in print?

# CHAPTER 11

B reakfast at the duke's table, in a room half the size of the formal dining room, seemed odd without the duke present. Even though they'd been at the castle for a fortnight with the head of the family still in London, Andrew couldn't help glancing at the head of the table, from time to time, where the duke normally sat.

Simon had kept his usual place to the right of the duke's chair, and Andrew couldn't blame him. It couldn't be easy for his friend, to know that one day he would lose his father and have to fill His Grace's shoes. Even after nearly a decade as baronet, Andrew still hesitated to enter the rooms his father had once called his own.

Josephine hadn't arrived at breakfast yet, but her sisters and their governess were in their usual places when the butler came into the room. He carried a silver tray, stacked high with folded missives. Invitations, letters, and solicitations for the ducal family.

"My lord, the post has arrived."

"Excellent. Is there anything from Their Graces in London?"

"Yes, my lord." The butler bowed as Simon accepted his correspondence. Then the butler made his way to Josephine's place, where he left a folded letter, then he delivered similar letters to the duke's other daughters. Finally, he made his way around the table to Andrew.

Andrew had a letter from his steward, as well as one from a friend in town asking him back to meet a cousin.

In the last few years, all his friends had started introducing him to their female relations. Usually under duress, with an aunt or mother forcing them to make those introductions. Thankfully, as a baronet, he wasn't in near as much demand as someone of Simon's standing.

He certainly had no interest in marriage at present. He could turn down the invitation without any remorse.

Simon interrupted Andrew's letter-reading, saying with the raised voice of one making an announcement, "Hartwell is coming for a visit."

The silence lasted half a breath. Then Simon's younger sisters started making high-pitched sounds of excitement that made Andrew wince.

"Lord Hartwell? Coming here?"

"While Mama and Papa are *away?*"

"Grandmama is here, silly. It's perfectly respectable."

"Oh, but he's so handsome."

"How long is he staying?"

Josephine drifted into the room as her sisters began a volley of questions.

"When will he arrive?"

"Is his younger brother coming too?"

"Will we see them, or are they only hunting?"

Andrew met Josephine's gaze as she arrived at her chair, her eyebrows raised. "What is all the excitement about?" She always sat beside him, and he across from Simon, at informal meals. The better that they might jab at one another with their words, if not their forks.

Her sisters chorused together, "Hartwell!"

Andrew watched Josephine's lips curl with amusement, then he turned to look at Simon. "I don't suppose they ever greet the news of my visits with such enthusiasm?"

Rosalind, the younger of the two schoolroom girls, snorted. "Of course not. You are like a brother to us."

He exchanged a sardonic look with Josephine. "I am not certain if that is meant to be a compliment or something else entirely."

"Then take it as a compliment," Josephine said, lowering herself into the chair a footman held out for her. "Simon, did you invite Hartwell?"

"I expected to see him in London, if we were still there, and I wrote only last week to tell him we had removed to the country." He held the letter across the table to his sister. "This arrived today. He said he'd rather be at the castle than in London anyway."

"That's a Yorker for you." Andrew looked over Josephine's arm to read the letter. "He'd rather be in his walled city than on the Thames." He spoke in jest, as he'd long counted Roman Eastwood, Baron Hartwell, a friend. The three of them—Simon, Roman, and Andrew—had gone to school together. In Roman Eastwood's first week at school, he'd been bullied mercilessly for his Yorkshire accent.

Andrew and Simon had intervened when one particularly vitriolic battle turned to fisticuffs, and the three had become fast friends. Roman had eventually shed the accent his Yorkshire upbringing had given him, adopting the "refined" elocution of the English upper ranks.

"I have been to York," Josephine said, handing him the letter. "It is a beautiful city, and certainly less crowded than London. I cannot fault him for enjoying himself there." She picked up the letter waiting for her and gasped. "It's from Emma! At last."

"She wrote you and not me?" Andrew asked, pretending to gaze at the letter with longing. "What of familial duty?"

"I sincerely doubt you want a letter from her that is doubtless filled with details of her honeymoon." Josephine lifted her fork and raised her eyebrow at him, but when Andrew only smirked, she realized what her words implied. Her cheeks turned a rosy hue he found most satisfying. "That is not—I did not mean—"

Mrs. Robinson, the governess, cleared her throat. "If you young ladies have finished your breakfasts, let us adjourn to the morning room for sewing and poetry."

Andrew kept his lips pressed together until the governess had withdrawn with her charges, and then he let himself laugh loud and long at Josephine's mortification.

Simon, for his part, barely glanced up from the letter he read as he said, "We all know what you meant, Josephine."

She stared gloomily at her plate, stabbing at a fried potato with vehemence. "Scold Sir Andrew if you must scold anyone."

Anytime she used formal address on him, Andrew knew he'd put himself in her black books. They'd gone days without much arguing—ever since he'd found her in the tower. It was something of a relief to see he could still tease a reaction from her, and with little effort.

"It isn't my place to scold anyone. Thank goodness." Simon put the paper down. "The girls are right, of course. Grandmother's presence, and mine, means that Hartwell's coming isn't at all indecent. But make certain your behavior is above reproach, all the same."

"Lord Hartwell doesn't care a ha'penny for me, Simon." Josephine made a dismissive gesture with the hand not holding an eating utensil. "He never has. And he is far better behaved than this one." She nodded to Andrew.

"Me?" Andrew protested, hand going to his chest as though wounded. "I am the very model of politeness and good manners."

She scoffed. "Perhaps in the medieval ages, where you would've made a fine jester."

Simon groaned. "Can we not go a quarter hour without you two badgering each other?" He folded his letter. "The point I am trying to make, Josephine, which you force me to speak plainly, is that this visit might be different from others. Particularly for you."

She blinked, and Andrew turned fully in his chair to face Simon. He could not mean—

Josephine spoke Andrew's very thought. "You do not mean Hartwell has another motive besides seeing you?" She sounded as shocked by the idea as Andrew felt. "Did Papa put him up to this?"

Andrew waited, watching as his friend folded his arms and leaned back in his chair.

"Father has nothing to do with this. Hartwell hasn't seen you in a few years, is all. You've grown up a bit. And I know he's started to consider marriage. I'm not saying that's his design in coming—because, so far as I know—it isn't. But what if the two of you like each other?"

Hartwell wouldn't be able to help noting all the ways Josephine had grown. She wasn't an adorable child anymore, but a beautiful woman. She was graceful. Intelligent. Compassionate. Kind. All things that a man of Hartwell's character would admire. All things that Andrew couldn't help admiring. But Hartwell had one benefit Andrew didn't—no one in the family thought of Hartwell as a brother. That would make it far easier for him to offer romance to Josephine than it would be for Andrew.

No. Andrew couldn't imagine it. Hartwell and Josephine? The two wouldn't suit at all. He relaxed into his chair and smirked over his shoulder at Josephine, burying his thoughts as deep as possible. "You could spend the entire time he's here hiding from him, like you did with Atella last autumn. That was most effective."

She gasped and tossed her napkin at him. "I didn't hide from Luca."

He raised his eyebrows and mouthed, knowing Simon couldn't see him, the word *tower*. Josephine's cheeks flamed, and her nostrils flared.

Continuing with little regard for his safety, Andrew added, "It is too bad you do not have another companion to throw at him. That worked out in Emma's favor, considering her new role as countess."

Josephine scowled at him, and Andrew could have sworn twin blue flames had appeared in her eyes. But instead of pitching his words back at him, her expression calmed. She turned her face to her brother and spoke with measured, polite tones. "I will make certain Lord Hartwell enjoys his time at Clairvoir. When do we expect him to arrive?"

Simon hesitated before speaking, perhaps sensing the same strangeness in the air as Andrew. "Four days from now."

"Very good. I will inform Grandmama of our coming guest." She stood from the table, her breakfast barely touched, snatched up the letter from Emma, and left the room at an unhurried pace.

When the door closed behind her, Andrew turned to look at Simon. "You cannot be serious. Hartwell and Josephine?"

Simon shrugged. "He's my friend and a good man. Why not?"

"I would say I am both those things, yet you wouldn't make a match of your sister and me." He snorted and watched his friend from the corner of his eye. Would Simon ever entertain that notion? He'd never suggested to Andrew, not so much as the barest of hints, that Andrew and Josephine might form an attachment to one another. And he didn't seem to care to address the matter at that moment, either.

"I'm not making matches of anyone," Simon said, pointedly not making eye contact with Andrew. "Merely presenting an opportunity to both of them. Hartwell is smart enough to take advantage of that opportunity. Whatever Josephine makes of it is her business. If she finds Hartwell suitable, I will not argue the point."

Though Andrew found he wanted to give a whole list of reasons why Hartwell wouldn't be suitable, he couldn't think of a single one. But he would. And Josephine would likely think of several. She'd avoided matchmaking mothers and gentlemen ever since her presentation at court three years before. As a duke's daughter, she could take all the time she wished before selecting a husband. She could likely wait until she turned eighty years old and still find plenty of men willing to marry her for her fortune alone.

He winced. Poor Josephine. How would she ever know if a man wanted her for herself or for her position?

Not that it should matter to him. Her family had things well in hand, and Josephine would never accept a match unless it was precisely what she wanted.

He shrugged, picked up his post, and followed Andrew to the duke's study. There, they would answer their letters of business before going out riding. And really—what better way to distract himself from thoughts of Josephine than spending his time on horseback?

JOSEPHINE KNOCKED AT THE DOOR OF HER GRANDMOTHER'S suite. Then she waited until her grandmother's companion, a new one pulled from the world of underprivileged and widowed second-cousins, opened the door.

"Mrs. Rollins, is my grandmother available?" Josephine asked kindly.

The middle-aged woman smiled as fondly as if Josephine had been her own grandchild. "Yes, of course, Lady Josephine. She is having her breakfast in bed, but you know that would never stop her from welcoming you."

Josephine followed Mrs. Rollins through the sitting room, decorated in her grandmother's favorite Egyptian style, and through to the airy bedchamber. The bed at the center of the room was one of the most important sticks of furniture in the castle. Family legend stated that King Henry VIII had once slept in that very bed when he came for a hunt with the Earl of Montfort in the sixteenth century.

No one in her family particularly cared for Henry VIII, but the ability to associate with royalty and history in any way somehow elevated one's standing in Society.

Her Grace, Sarah, the Duchess of Montfort, certainly looked queenly in her lace cap and purple shawl. A tray of breakfast was at her side, with more on a table near her should she wish for something other than her usual favorites.

"Josephine," she said with a welcome smile. "Why are you not downstairs at breakfast?"

"Everyone finished early. Today's post sent everyone into raptures." She didn't bother hiding her crooked smile. Her grandmother could be a bit of a dragon, but Josephine found her more amusing than intimidating.

"I see no reason a bit of mail should keep young people from eating properly. Take some toast, dear. Or bacon. And tea."

Though she had left the table without an appetite, making her way to her grandmother's rooms had restored her desire for food. She made herself a small plate, then sat in a chair beside her grandmother's bed. Her grandmother's companion remained in the adjoining sitting room, giving them privacy.

"I have had my own letter today, from your mother. She writes that all is well in London, though she misses her daughters' company. She went to the most intriguing lecture at the palace." The dowager duchess went on to describe her daughter-in-law's letter, giving Josephine time to enjoy her second attempt at breakfast.

When Josephine finished her last bite of toast, her grandmother finally said, "I cannot help but wonder, my dear, whom it was that wrote something to excite everyone."

"Oh. That." Josephine's shoulders dropped, but she snapped them back into place at once. Grandmother couldn't abide poor posture in young people. "Lord Hartwell wrote that he is coming to visit."

"Hartwell? He's Simon's friend, isn't he? That Yorkshire baron."

"The very one." She traced the edge of her plate with one finger, avoiding her grandmother's gaze.

"Good. He is a lively young man. And rather nice to look at."

A startled laugh escaped from Josephine, then she gasped. "Grandmama!"

"I may be old, dear girl." Her grandmother tipped her nose in the air. "But there is nothing wrong with my eyesight." A tart retort rose to Josephine's lips, but good sense meant she kept them closed. "I suppose your sisters squealed happily, your brother warned you to be on your best behavior, and Sir Andrew glowered."

"Right on almost every account." Josephine rose and gathered her grandmother's plate on top of her own. "But why would Sir Andrew *glower*? He's as much a friend to Hartwell as Simon." She turned to stack both plates on the tray.

"Jealousy, of course."

Josephine peered over her shoulder at her grandmother. "For Simon's attention? I do not think he is so needy a friend as that." She gave her attention to the teapot, checking the small candle beneath that kept it warm, then poured her grandmother a fresh cup of tea.

Her grandmother chuckled. "I quite agree with you. The man is independent of everyone. I think perhaps that is one reason he cannot determine what he most needs."

"It is not like you to speak in riddles." Josephine brought her grandmother the tea. "In less than a minute's time, you have said Andrew is jealous, independent, and needful."

As she accepted her cup and saucer, the dowager duchess

indulged in a superior sniff. "Indeed. And I hope you were listening." Then her grandmother changed the subject, asking after Josephine's itinerary for the day.

A quarter of an hour later, Josephine withdrew to her bedroom to read her letter from Emma. She sat on the large windowsill, angling the letter to the light, and read with eagerness.

*My Friend,*

*I cannot tell you the depth of my disappointment when I arrived in London only to learn you had returned to the country. I visited with your mother at once, and when I understood the circumstances, I mourned your absence. My dear husband shares the duke's concern. The unrest in London continues to mount. Though Luca suggested sending me to Clairvoir, I insisted I remain by his side, as the duchess remains with the duke. The only difficult thing I face in making that decision is missing you, dearest. I hope you understand.*

*I received your letter. You hint that your writing has undergone an important change? I understand your reason for subterfuge— one never knows what may happen to a personal letter—but I cannot give you sound advice until we make the matter clear. I hope to come to the castle when Parliament adjourns for the Season. Hold all your lovely news until then!*

*Luca and I enjoyed our time away. Marriage is everything I hoped it would be....*

The letter continued in Emma's fine hand, painting a picture of marital happiness that pressed against Josephine's heart. Her eyes grew damp, the tears a mixture of sorrow for losing her dearest companion and joy that her friend had found the love of her life.

Emma no longer needed Josephine as she had before. Of course, they would forever be friends, and as dear to one another as sisters. But the relationship between husband and wife would

forever be deeper and more important than one friend to another.
Emma had Luca.

Who did Josephine have?

# CHAPTER 12

When Roman Eastwood arrived on the promised day, the household turned upside down to greet him. At least, that's how it seemed. Josephine had spent the morning reassuring her sisters that their gowns were acceptable and—yes—made them look quite grown up. Then she endured another lecture from Simon on being attentive to their guest. Her grandmother had exchanged a knowing look with her in the salon when her sisters did not deviate from the subject of their guest. Then the dowager duchess smirked to herself the rest of the day.

When the time came at last to gather in the foyer, their Guard Room, to greet Lord Hartwell and his younger brother, Josephine edged closer to Andrew in hopes of speaking to someone still in possession of their senses.

Andrew glanced at her when she took her place at his side, then adjusted the cuff of his coat. "I cannot say I have ever received a welcome such as this. Ought I to be flattered or insulted?"

She had to press her lips together a moment to avoid smirking. Was this what her grandmother meant when she assumed Andrew was jealous of Lord Hartwell? She schooled her features into something superior. "We never make a fuss over *you* because you are as good as one of the family. Is that worthy of insult?"

He appeared to consider, and when she raised her eyebrows, he chuckled. "I suppose not." He nudged her shoulder with his. "You needn't listen to Simon, you know. If you don't like Hartwell, there's no reason to pretend he might suit."

Heat flooded her cheeks. Speaking of this with her family was one thing, but Andrew? He hadn't ever teased her about her suitors before.

"It really is none of your business," she said, and then turned her attention to the long entry hall. The carriage had finally arrived in the vestibule.

Andrew bent toward her, lowering his voice to speak directly into her ear while Rosalind and Isabelle giggled on her other side. "Anyone could see you weren't happy with Simon's suggestion that Hartwell is here to see you." As he spoke, his breath whispered across her neck, warm and familiar. Her stomach dipped oddly.

Josephine leaned away and glared up at him. "Perhaps 'anyone' ought not to speak on the subject when it is none of their affair."

A deep-throated bark sounded, echoing through the hall, startling Josephine and Andrew both. She looked down the corridor again.

Roman Eastman, Lord Hartwell, strode down the hall with his brother at his right and two large dogs flanking them on either side. Massive dogs, the likes of which she had not seen before. They had to be some sort of boar hound, given they appeared large-chested and not fleet of foot like a deerhound.

Lord Hartwell and Lyness, his brother, were both quite handsome. They were tall, though not so tall as Simon or the duke, and carried themselves with all the confidence of men nobly born. Simon stepped forward to greet them properly, and the dogs sat in unison as their master bowed.

"Lord Farleigh," Hartwell said, his voice low and not entirely unpleasant. He grinned broadly. "It's good to be at Clairvoir again."

"It's been an age," Simon agreed, then turned to Lyness. "Welcome, Mr. Eastwood."

Lyness bowed again. He was four and twenty, his elder brother eight and twenty. They were alike in appearance in most respects, except the baron had blue eyes and his younger brother brown. "Mother sends her regrets," Lyness said. "She is in Bath, visiting a friend in poor health."

"We will miss her, but I am certain she is exactly where she needs to be," the dowager duchess said, and both visitors bowed deeply to her.

Everyone was reintroduced, and Andrew managed not to linger over Josephine and Hartwell's interaction, brief as it was. Isabelle and Rosalind, despite their obvious infatuation, did not to giggle, or tip over when they curtsied.

Josephine's curiosity overcame her, and she asked Lyness as their older brothers made small talk about the roads, "What sort of dogs are those? They are quite massive."

Lyness grinned and made a gesture with his hand to one of the canines. It rose from where it sat and came to his side, its docked tail wagging furiously. "He is a Danish boarhound. This is Apollo, and his mate, Athena. Roman is training them as guards and companions, instead of leaving them to the kennels where such massive beasts belong."

Lord Hartwell interrupted his conversation with her brother, leaning toward them as he answered. "There is no practical reason for ladies to have their pugs with them at all times, either. So long as they are well behaved, why banish them from the house?"

Josephine eyed the massive dog at her feet, looking into its large eyes and imagining the enormity of its teeth. "An unusual idea, for hunting dogs. Does your kennel master not train them as you wish?"

"My kennel master is among the best," Lord Hartwell said, unoffended. "Which is why my dogs are more suitable to a castle than some gentlemen are." He came closer and laid his hand atop the dog's head. "You may pet him, if you like, my lady."

Josephine hesitated. Though not normally afraid of animals, there was something to say about a dog who—when sitting—was more than half her height. Then she held out her hand for the animal to sniff before putting it between his ears. The creature leaned into her touch, its eyes large and soulful. She couldn't help smiling.

"There you are. Fast friends," Lord Hartwell said, scratching beneath the dog's chin. He stood quite near, and yet Josephine felt neither stirred by his nearness nor repelled. She kept herself from sighing aloud.

Lord Hartwell wasn't for her. No matter what her brother wished.

The servants whisked the visiting brothers away to show them their rooms, their massive dogs with them. Her grandmother, sisters, and their governess went away, whispering quietly about their guests.

Andrew reappeared by her side, looking at her askance. "There now." He smiled, though it was brief. "What do you think? Does the baron have a chance with the duke's daughter?"

Irritated as she was with all the matchmaking machinations of her family, Andrew joining the fray was more than she would countenance. But rather than narrow her eyes at him and answer sharply—which would only encourage his teasing—she pursed her lips as though giving the matter serious thought. She may as well have a bit of fun.

"Hartwell isn't the worst candidate I have considered, though it remains to be seen if he is the best." Josephine tapped her chin with a single finger. "I suppose more time in his company will help me put the matter to rest." She spoke in cheerful tones. "His affection for animals is quite telling of his character, is it not?"

Then she walked away from Andrew, only glancing back when she had gained the stairs.

He remained where she left him, a perplexing frown in place of his usual relaxed expression.

NEVER HAD ANDREW SEEN SUCH REMARKABLY WELL-trained dogs as Apollo and Athena. The animals accompanied the four men on their morning ride, the day after Hartwell and his brother arrived at Castle Clairvoir. They kept up with the horses and never strayed far from their master's watchful eyes.

It might surprise the duchess to see such enormous dogs trotting around her castle behind the baron, granted as much free rein as a lady's lapdog or a terrier.

Was it wrong of Andrew to hope she returned to the castle while the baron remained? He should very much like to see how she reacted to the monstrous beasts lying upon her rugs. Even if they were perhaps the smartest dogs he had ever seen.

The men had halted at a rise overlooking Lambsthorpe, which was alive with people going about their morning chores and errands. Andrew smiled to himself, thinking of when he and Josephine had confused anyone watching with their walk to and from the vicarage a fortnight past.

"What is your opinion, Hartwell?" Simon's voice brought Andrew away from his thoughts. "I know it is early yet, but you must at least have an impression of her already."

Andrew's gut twisted. He kept still, not turning to see what Roman Eastman's expression might tell him. At dinner the evening before, he had been moved from his usual place next to Josephine to allow the guest of honor to sit in that place. He'd sat between the dowager and Lyness, instead, and had only caught snatches of the conversation between Josephine and the baron.

At breakfast, he had arrived late. Sleep had eluded him the

night previous. When he came to the table, it was to see the baron assisting Josephine from the table. Then the man had walked out of the room with her, and neither had returned.

"Do you know how strange it is, for a brother to ask a man what he thinks of a sister?" Hartwell asked, amusement in his tone. He whistled a command to the dogs, who had bounded like puppies down the hill. They stopped, turned, and loped back up toward the riders. "I think she has grown into a charming young woman, but I am not ready to say whether we might be a match for one another."

"You know how Roman is," Lyness said, and this time Andrew looked. The younger man wore a wide grin. "He is notoriously slow at making decisions. He must ruminate a fortnight at least before he changes his menu. It will take him at least a year of such contemplation on the subject of matrimony. Maybe two."

Why did that declaration give Andrew leave to relax the tension in his shoulders? Tension that had been building ever since Roman Eastman's arrival. The relief was short-lived.

"I doubt it will take so long as that. Marriage is an important decision. The most essential decision, I should think, one will make in life. While I have no intention of rushing into it, I certainly will not hesitate to offer for a woman if I believe her to be the companion of my heart." The baron spoke with such solemnity that his brother said no more, and Simon nodded gravely, as though he approved of the baron's words.

The words had cast a spell over them all, apparently. Even Andrew felt their effects. The companion of his heart. He'd never thought long enough about marriage to put such words to what many of his peers called "leg-shackling" and "end to freedom."

Hartwell hadn't struck Andrew as the romantic sort. Yet he spoke as though it was something to aspire to rather than make trite witticisms about. And the baron meant to find out if Josephine would be that lifelong companion to him. Not just a feather in his cap, a social connection, or a dowry. But a part of his heart.

Simon spoke about the village, pointing here and there to improvements he and his father planned. Hartwell listened raptly, and Lyness hung back with Andrew.

"My brother is serious about finding a wife," Lyness said, pulling Andrew's attention to him.

"I have no doubt." Andrew dismounted under the pretense of checking Honey's foreleg. He scraped off dried mud and smoothed down the hair on the horse's leg.

"I thought I should say something. You didn't look best pleased with the idea." Lyness dismounted, too. He picked up a long stick from the grass and threw it to the back of the hill for Apollo and Athena to chase. Each dog grabbed an end of the stick and playfully tried to tug it away from the other. "I know you are a close friend to the family, but perhaps you don't see Roman the way I do. You shouldn't worry that he will toy with Lady Josephine's affections."

"Of course not." Andrew hadn't meant the words to come out as clipped and irritable as they had. He gritted his teeth, then forced a pleasant countenance back in place. "Hartwell is an honorable man. If the duke thinks him an appropriate suitor, why would I worry?"

He mounted Honey again.

*Why worry indeed.* Everything Hartwell and Lyness said ought to have reassured Andrew. He was content to act as a brother to Josephine, wasn't he? He'd decided that's all he could be when he returned from Ireland to find a woman grown in place of the quick-witted child he had teased.

That moment in the rain came back to him, flooding his mind with the scent of the air, the glow of her eyes. They had stood so close. Closer than he'd ever seen Simon stand with his sister. He'd faced her. Bent enough to peer beneath her bonnet as the rain fell around them. Barely more than a hands' breadth between them as they spoke. The world had gone still and soft, the only sound the rush of his pulse in his ears, her soft breath, and the patter of rain upon the leaves.

Apollo barked, and Honey twitched away from the overly large dog, plunging Andrew back into the present moment.

"I think it's time to return to the castle," Simon said. "I have matters to attend to. Perhaps my sisters will keep you company while I am busy." He grinned at Hartwell, then Andrew, who returned the smile briefly.

Why had Andrew's stomach turned sour? Why, as they pointed their horses toward the castle again, did he catch himself glaring at the back of Hartwell's head as they rode?

The sky above may well have been clear, but a cloud of vexation encompassed his thoughts. A storm brewed within, and Andrew hadn't any idea when, or if, it would thunder to life.

# CHAPTER 13

T wo days of puzzling over the matter of Lord Hartwell and Josephine as a possible match had brought Andrew no closer to understanding why such an idea bothered him. The amount of thought he put into the subject had left him tired—as had the late evenings at billiards and discussing politics with the other men in the castle. Which meant he had slept in on the third day of the Eastwoods' visit and subsequently missed breakfast.

He went to the library, thinking nothing of the meal, and took one of the couches as his own. Book in hand, he stretched out along the cushions without the least bit of care for the impolite posture.

The only person at home in the castle who might scold him for such a thing was the dowager duchess. And she never came into the library. She always sent her companion or a grandchild to fetch her books for her.

Andrew made an effort to read. Truly. But the words on the page blurred when his thoughts went elsewhere. Or he found himself reading the same paragraph again and again without comprehending what it meant.

He finally groaned and dropped the book on himself, his nose pinched by the stitched binding and the covers forming a tent over his face.

The library door opened with a click. He didn't move. Let whoever it was get their book and then leave him in alone.

"Josephine? Are you in here? Josephine—Sir Andrew!" His name came out with the same force one might use to scold a dog found chewing on the furniture.

He sat up, the book falling to the cushion beside him, then jumped all the way to his feet when he saw Her Grace, the dowager duchess, glaring at him. "Your Grace, I beg your pardon."

"You ought to beg the couch's pardon. What sort of gentleman puts his shoes on the furniture?" She tsked at him. "The moment I think you boys have matured, I find Simon sliding down a banister or you leaping upon the furniture."

Simon hadn't slid down a banister since they were thirteen, Andrew well knew, and he certainly hadn't been leaping on furniture. Ever. But he kept those protests to himself and apologized instead. "Forgive me, Your Grace." He added a bow for good measure. "That was a terrible lapse in manners." Then, as she had suggested, he turned and bowed to the couch. He spoke with the same sincere tone he had used to address her. "Forgive me, furniture, for mistreating you."

The duchess clucked, and when he faced her, he saw the amusement in her eyes. Dragon she may be, but Andrew hadn't ever doubted her affection for her grandchildren. Or for him. "You are a silly young man."

"And you are a saint for putting up with me, Your Grace."

She dismissed his comment with an elegant flick of her wrist. "Nevermind that. Have you seen Josephine? I have sent servants searching through the house for her, but she has yet to appear. I thought if I wished to find her, I would have to do it myself."

Andrew knew immediately where the lady had gone. Her tower. Where else would she disappear to without being found?

Unless she'd left the castle again. But no, she had promised, and Josephine didn't break promises.

The dowager duchess folded her hands before her. "There—you know where she is. I can tell by the look on your face."

He hesitated, then rocked back on his heels. "I might know."

"You do. Sir Andrew, tell me at once. Where is my grand-daughter?" The woman had an air of command that most generals would envy, if not the king himself. Her graying hair didn't make her mind, tongue, or eyes any less sharp.

He drew himself up. "I cannot tell you, Your Grace."

"Cannot?" she repeated, raising her eyebrows high. "Or will not?"

"Both, Your Grace." This would make her an enemy for certain, at least for a fortnight. "Though I can assure you Lady Josephine is safe, within the castle walls. I have promised to keep the knowledge of her whereabouts to myself. So, you see, it is a matter of honor."

Her wide eyes narrowed, and the wrinkles around her mouth deepened as she pursed her lips. "You promised Josephine you would not tell me, her *grandmother,* where she is hiding?"

"I promised I would tell no one where she takes herself when she wishes to be alone."

"And how did you come across this hidden hole of hers?"

"Quite by accident, I assure you."

"Humph." The dowager duchess strode to the windows over-looking the courtyard. "She is neglecting our guests. Do tell her I said so when you see her, Sir Andrew. You may also tell her I am both displeased and impressed with your ability to keep her confi-dences." Then she turned and strode from the room, regal as an empress, without saying another word to him.

His shoulders fell, and he stared after the dowager duchess in shock, but moments after she vanished from the doorway, one of the guardsmen-playing-footman appeared. Sterling, one of the duke's favorites.

The guard bowed, then returned to his soldier-stiff stance. "Sir Andrew. As a servant to His Grace, I must ask that you reveal Lady Josephine's whereabouts to me. I am under orders to keep the family safe."

"The family *is* safe." Andrew sighed and rubbed at his temple. "Josephine is in the castle, and so long as she is within its walls, you needn't be her shadow. Correct?"

The guardsman appeared uncertain. "That is true. However, my position requires that I know each member of the family is protected. I understand and honor your promise to my lady. I ask instead that you ensure she is where you think her to be, and if she is not, that you find myself or one of the other guardsmen immediately, so we might search her out."

Andrew couldn't fault the man for fulfilling his duty. Josephine would have to endure another invasion of her haven. "That is acceptable."

The guard bowed in thanks, then withdrew. Andrew picked up his book from where it had fallen, then left the library. To ensure he wasn't followed, Andrew wove through the castle as carefully as possible. He went through multiple rooms, even down to the kitchens, where he liberated several small items from the pantries. Then he slipped through servants' hidden halls, and finally darted into the closet that concealed the entrance to the tower.

Though he'd never admit it, not even to himself, an excuse to look in on Josephine had been precisely what he was waiting for.

FINDING A MOMENT TO SLIP AWAY TO HER TOWER HADN'T been easy for Josephine. Not for the last two days. Finally, she decided the only thing for it was to take no more than toast for breakfast and leave the dining room before anyone else had entered it.

The clock she had taken from the corner of a room where no one noticed it kept her abreast of the time. Everyone else would have finished breakfast an hour or more ago, and she had been hard at work on her manuscript for nearly two hours.

When she heard a noise from the stairs, she stilled the scratching of her quill. Then looked at it with a scowl. Bother the pens. She ought to have bought one of the newer variety in London when she had the chance. She was quite tired of repairing her instrument and would use pencil were it tidier.

"Josephine?" Andrew's voice startled a blush from her, and it preceded him into the tower room. She looked up from her work but did not rise from her cushions. She tucked her feet closer.

"I am here."

Andrew emerged from the staircase wearing a grin and carrying a cloth bundle. "I knew you were here."

She arched an eyebrow at him. "Had you any great need to find me? I cannot imagine one."

Andrew sat without waiting for an invitation, taking the same place as before, against the stone between two stained glass windows. "Your grandmother set everyone in the household to looking for you."

"Oh." Josephine put down her pen and clutched her shawl closer to her shoulders. The tower was somewhat cold this morning. "I did not think my company was wanted this morning."

"There's an eligible nobleman in the castle," Andrew said, tone suspiciously light. "Of course the dowager duchess wishes you present."

"Bother. Does that mean I need to go to my grandmother?" She prepared to stand, gathering her skirts in hand.

"I made your excuses," he said, looking away from her. "And I might have told her I knew where you were."

Her skin prickled, and everything went cold. "You promised you wouldn't tell anyone—"

"And I didn't," he rushed to say, making a calming motion

SALLY BRITTON

with one hand. "No one knows your precise location. But I had to reassure her, so she did not send out a search party. The guards were also concerned. I thought Sterling might try to force your location out of me."

She covered her mouth with one hand. "So you told everyone—"

"Your grandmother and Sterling," he corrected.

Josephine put as much fierceness in her glare as she could, but the panic bubbling up in her chest was no less palpable. "You told both of them, which might as well have meant announcing it from the ramparts, that you know where I disappear to? When no one else does?"

He shifted uncomfortably. "It was that or let them keep looking for you until they'd grown frenzied with worry. No one knows where you are for certain, only that you are safe inside the castle."

"You revealed to Grandmother that I have a place I go," she said, hearing her voice edge into a higher register than she'd ever used before. "When she sees me next, she will demand to know where, and then I'll never be able to use the tower again, and—"

Andrew left his bundle behind and moved from where he sat across the floor to kneel in front of her. He put one hand on her shoulder and cupped her chin with the other, guiding her to look at him. His brow was etched with concern, his eyes dark with worry. "Josie. Take a breath. Listen."

She pressed her lips together and stared at him, her heart aching with the loss of the only place in the castle she felt was truly her own. She tried to follow back the bitter taste of disappointment on her tongue.

"You needn't tell anyone where you go. You are in the castle. Tucked away in a quiet corner. If they press you for answers, you need only say that you are sorry you worried them, but you needn't disclose your location to anyone unless you wish it."

"Grandmama will tell Father," Josephine whispered, her eyes

burning with tears. She couldn't cry in front of Andrew. He'd never let her hear the last of it—except she had cried in front of him that day in the rain. And he'd never mentioned it.

Andrew's voice softened. "Your father is the most reasonable man I know. I cannot imagine him intruding upon you here, even if you told him where you spend your time." His thumb brushed her cheek near the corner of her mouth, then he slowly withdrew his hands and moved away. "Don't borrow trouble until it comes."

She sniffled and searched about for her handkerchief. "That is much easier for you to say than for me to do."

"Josie." Andrew held his large white handkerchief out to her. "Stop fretting. Your secret is still safe."

Perhaps he was right. Her father hadn't ever treated his children heavy-handed, despite being a duke. She dabbed at her eyes with the cloth Andrew provided, then sighed. "I don't suppose I expected to have it all to myself forever. What a childish thing. Like when boys make their ridiculous 'clubs' in attics and outbuildings."

"The clubs in London are as ridiculous," Andrew told her with complete seriousness. "Why do we always look for places to hide ourselves away from things?"

She shrugged one shoulder and leaned against the stone wall. "I cannot speak for anyone but myself. I suppose I am here because I want a place that is my own." Her throat tightened, and she looked to Andrew, measuring his response to her words. "Is that ridiculous for me to say, given who I am?"

Andrew settled in his place again and stretched out his legs before him, crossing them at the ankles and looking for all the world as comfortable as a man on a picnic. "I imagine writers would need a quiet place to think, and to write undisturbed. The last time I tried writing a letter in the Rose Salon, I was interrupted half a dozen times by people pestering me with questions about what I was writing." He appeared heartily disgusted by the memory and then broke into a smile. "Is that what you mean?"

"I meant because I am a duke's daughter." Josephine looked down at her traveling desk, the pen and paper atop it appearing as nothing more than innocent tools. "I live in a castle."

"Your father's castle, full of family, guests, and servants. Taking time to yourself is not a horrible thing." Andrew picked up his bundle and unwrapped it, revealing the cloth as a large linen napkin, and its contents.

"Food," Josephine said, eyes wide. "But what of mice?"

"Up here?" he shrugged. "We will be careful not to leave so much as a crumb behind." He offered her a roll and an apple. "Are you hungry?"

Her empty stomach twisted unhappily. She took the apple and soft round roll from him. "Thank you. Did you bring any for yourself?"

"Are you inviting me to stay?" Was it her imagination, or did he seem hopeful as he asked that absurd question?

"Of course. I cannot have you leaving at the wrong moment and giving away my position."

One corner of his mouth went higher than the other when he smiled, and a gleam of amusement appeared in his eyes. "I thought as much. There is enough for two of us to enjoy a small repast."

He took an apple in one hand and reached into his waistcoat with the other, pulling out a slim book which he opened. He leaned back and started reading without another word, taking a large bite of his apple before turning the page.

Josephine watched him as she nibbled at the bread, waiting for him to begin a conversation. But when he remained quiet, even after he'd finished his apple and she hers, she put her desk upon her lap again and took up her quill pen. Only then did he look up from the pages of his book.

"Would you like me to leave, so you can write in peace?"

"No." The answer surprised her almost as much as it seemed to surprise him. "I do not mind—and you will have a quiet place to read. If you wish to stay, that is." She ducked her head and dipped her quill in the inkwell, ignoring the way her cheeks grew warm. Had she sounded foolish to him, or only to herself?

"Thank you." Andrew didn't complicate the matter with more words than that. He picked up his book, and the two remained together in the sunlit tower. Quietly keeping each other from being alone.

# CHAPTER 14

When Josephine appeared in the sitting room before dinner, Grandmama surprised her by *not* asking where she had hidden away. Though she hinted heavily that Josephine better not disappear the next day.

That meant when morning came, Josephine lingered at the breakfast table with the others, and she accepted an invitation to ride with the gentlemen when her brother extended it. Despite preferring to stay inside, working on her book. Or perhaps reading one. The time spent quietly in Andrew's company the day before had surprised her. It had been peaceful. Restorative, even.

Instead of giving in to her wishes, Josephine spent the morning comporting herself as a proper young lady, riding side-saddle, and most certainly *not* thinking of riding in the rain. That last was quite difficult considering the expressions Andrew sent her way every time their eyes met.

Given the way he grinned, smirked, and teased as ever he had, he certainly didn't think on that day as often as she did, or with the same strange muddle of emotion. Or as often as she tried *not* to relive the moments when her shoulder pressed against his chest and his arm encircled her waist.

She only thought on those things—she told herself firmly—in regard to how she might apply them to her new story, should the heroine ever find herself in an embrace with the hero.

Not that she thought of Andrew as any sort of hero.

Botheration. Why was her mind in such a muddle?

When Andrew finally moved ahead of her, riding next to Lyness Eastman, Josephine relaxed somewhat. At least he wouldn't catch her watching his form and noting his fine seat—no one rode a horse with as much ease as Sir Andrew Wycomb. Something she wouldn't ever admit to admiring. Especially to him.

"It's a fine sight, isn't it?"

Josephine blinked rapidly as she looked to Lord Hartwell. Obviously, he didn't mean what *she* had been staring at. He was staring out over the fields dotted with sheep. "Yes. Quite a lovely sight in the spring."

"I don't spend as much time in the country as I probably should. Our family home is so near York." He shrugged dismissively and then turned his sky-blue eyes in her direction. Her sisters were quite right; Baron Hartwell was handsome, but she felt no compulsion to blush or titter in response to his attention.

It was as she suspected. She simply had no desire to marry at present, no matter how handsome the man who appeared before her.

"I understand your mother has beautiful gardens, though. She is rather famous for her roses, isn't she?"

His eyes noticeably brightened. "She has attempted to collect specimens from all over England, to unite them in her gardens. Including the York and Lancaster Rose, which she could speak about at length. I recommend never bringing it up unless you wish for a combined history and botany lesson."

"I will make a note of that, my lord." Though she didn't plan on seeing the baroness anytime in the near future. The baron's mother famously never left her county. "I suppose you do not share your mother's interest in flowers. That is a shame. Our gardens have come along quite well since the last time you visited."

The baron's eyebrows raised nearly to his hat's brim. "I have as much interest as any other man in green and growing things."

"That would mean almost none." Josephine hadn't any intention of teasing him, but the words came out sounding far too friendly even to her ears. She fidgeted with the wrist of her glove and tried to sound neutral when she spoke again. "You should tour ours, though. If nothing else, to give you something to tell your mother of when you return home."

"I would be happy to take a tour through them, if you are volunteering to be the guide." He made no pretense of looking away or behaving with any sort of shyness. Instead, he grinned at her most boldly. As though he understood something she did not. "Though I imagine I can find plenty of other things about my visit to discuss with my mother."

Oh dear. Perhaps he had mistaken her intent. But now she could not withdraw what he had assumed she meant as an invitation without being rude. "Of course. I would be delighted to show you our flowers."

This was why she needed a companion. Emma would not have let Josephine stumble into this situation. Emma would have changed the subject or found a way around the unmeant invitation entirely. But Emma was far away in London, happily making a home with her husband.

A pang of loneliness struck Josephine's heart. She had nearly forgotten how much she missed Emma. Her gaze traveled ahead, tracing the lines of hilltop and treetop, then falling to the horizon —where Andrew's dark eyes and concerned expression captured her.

"Lady Josephine?" From the way Hartwell spoke her name, it wasn't the first time he had tried to catch her attention.

"Hm? I am sorry, my lord. My mind was rather caught up in

the beauty of the scenery." She gestured vaguely in the direction of the castle. "What was that you said?"

He didn't appear at all put out by her inattention, which would be a mark in his favor if she entertained the notion of accepting a suitor. Which she did not. "I asked if tomorrow afternoon would be an appropriate time for our garden tour." His horse danced sideways, flicking its ears nervously.

Andrew would say the beast had picked up on its rider's emotions, but as Lord Hartwell appeared perfectly at ease, she doubted that was the case.

"Thank you, yes. My schedule certainly allows for it." Josephine kept her smile polite and her tone as close to indifferent as she could. There was no use in raising the man's hopes.

Andrew had circled back, bringing his horse alongside hers. "Hartwell. Lady Josephine." At least he could mind his manners enough to call her by her title before others. "Had enough for one day?"

"Not at all," Josephine answered, unable to resist returning his grin. "Unless, of course, *you* are too tired to continue?"

"Me?" Andrew's horse danced sideways beneath him, then knickered. "As you can see, Honey and I are quite capable of going for hours yet."

"Hours?" Lord Hartwell sounded only mildly amused by the idea. "The two of you might have the wherewithal for that, but I vote for a return to the castle sooner rather than later."

Josephine returned to her polite indifference. "I suppose that would be for the best."

"But perhaps we might race back?" Andrew presented.

Quite familiar with Andrew's racing technique, Josephine raised one eyebrow at him. "You will want to wager, I suppose?"

"Always."

Lord Hartwell chuckled, but Josephine didn't even glance at him as he spoke. "I didn't take you for a gambling man."

"I never wager more than I can afford to lose," Andrew said with an easy shrug.

"And the prize is almost never coin," Josephine added. "What did you have in mind this time?"

"The last one to the castle must serve the others tea."

It took more than a little control to avoid snorting in amusement. "That is hardly a decent forfeit."

"I thought to keep it mild, for the sake of our guest, who is unfamiliar with our ways." Andrew had the audacity to wink at her before turning his grin to Hartwell. "We wouldn't want to shock you."

How many times had Andrew said "we" and "our" about the two of them in the last moment? And why hadn't she caught it until the last? She laughed, the sound weak to her own ears. "Sir Andrew, Simon, and myself have long teased one another this way. Do not worry much over our ridiculousness, Lord Hartwell."

The baron stared at her with a furrowed brow, clearly contemplating the scene before him and the actors in it too closely for her comfort. He must think her peculiar to go along with Andrew's odd scheme.

But before she could withdraw from the idea, Andrew snapped his fingers. "I have it. Tea will be served, as I said. But the person pouring out must also wear one of the frilled aprons the maids all wear."

The idea of Andrew in an apron serving her tea appealed to her, but she chewed her bottom lip and looked to the baron. "While I have no wish to disparage your riding abilities, Lord Hartwell, I do not think the terms fair to you, a guest in my home."

He quirked an eyebrow upward. "My sense of honor is uninjured, my lady. And I cannot imagine the ruffles on an apron would suit me poorly. Of course, I'd much rather Sir Andrew serve the two of us tea."

The baron went up in her estimation with that easy declaration. There were few men in the world willing to look silly, especially for the sake of something so small. Perhaps she might befriend the baron after all.

"Very well. As no one has any objections, let us inform the others and invite them to participate. I should hate to leave out Simon or Lyness." Andrew whirled his horse about and trotted down the path where the other men had paused to wait for those who had fallen behind.

Josephine shook her head somewhat ruefully. "We will all be sorry if Andrew wins. He will crow about it for days."

Hartwell chuckled. "But imagine if he is the one who loses."

"You are a good sport, to participate even under threat of wearing a maid's apron." Josephine didn't try to hide her admiration of that fact. "I cannot think of many gentlemen I know who would chance such a thing."

"My pride can stand it." He walked his horse around hers, his eyes sparkling at her. "Can yours?"

There ought to have been something—she instinctively knew it was missing—that happened when a man looked at a woman like that. She should have felt her stomach twist, or her heart race, or a blush grow in her cheeks. But instead, she felt only the same amusement she would if her own brother teased her.

It was quite disappointing. Even Andrew stirred up unusual sensations now and again.

That thought, unbidden as it was, made her jolt in the saddle. Her horse side-stepped and flicked an ear back at her. Josephine hastily soothed the beast with a hum of nonsense and a pat on the neck.

Andrew couldn't *stir* her feelings. Not unless he drove her to distraction with his absurd behavior, or to anger with his irritating teasing. Those were the only sorts of feelings he inspired—negative ones.

Then Andrew appeared beside her. The clack of horseshoes from behind meant Simon and Lyness Eastwood followed.

Andrew's wide grin, infectious as it was, didn't quite penetrate the sudden fog of confusion in her thoughts.

"Are you ready, Josie?"

She blinked, trying to focus on him. On the sparkle in his eye. The lift of his lips. The strangely endearing tilt to his head.

"O-of course." She cleared her throat self-consciously and forced herself to sit straight again. Imperious to all. "But I must ask you a very important question first."

His amusement grew. "And what would that be?"

"Do you remember how I take my tea?" She batted her eyelashes at him, then nudged her horse forward to the gate that would mark a perfect starting line. She heard Andrew's chuckle, low and deep, behind her.

ANDREW WASN'T A FOOL. HE'D NETTLED JOSEPHINE, THOUGH he hadn't thought his challenge distasteful. He knew Hartwell from school, just as Simon did, and the three of them had used to get up to far more embarrassing capers.

But something about the way she looked at him when he returned, jolly as he was that everyone meant to take part, warned him that something made Josephine uneasy.

He never second-guessed his interactions with her. They knew each other too well to worry over taking a jest too far, even if she did act put out by him from time to time. He always caught the edge of her smile when she would turn away from him. And he liked making her smile. Especially of late, with the frustration and fear over the unrest in London.

The five of them, four men and Josephine, lined up along the open gate. They would race along the main path back to the stables, rather than uphill to the castle. Racing up the steep incline wouldn't be kind to their mounts, and Andrew would never encourage something that would bring harm to a horse.

"We will let the lady call the start," Andrew declared as all of them bent over their horse's back.

Josephine, despite riding sidesaddle, was a force to be reckoned with when she rode. He had seen her take jumps that other ladies would never even consider.

"We proceed on three," she shouted. "One. Two. Three!"

The horses leaped forward, and the five of them were off. The narrowness of the road meant they would have to work to pass one another, but the course they had set was no more than a mile long.

Josephine took an early lead, and Andrew kept behind her. As Simon passed on Andrew's right, he wore a smile larger than Andrew had seen in some time. The worry over his parents in London had kept both the duke's eldest children from their usual cheer. If the race did nothing more than grant them a reprieve from that anxiety, Andrew would be pleased enough.

The dogs kept with the groom that had followed them out, which meant the horses could run freely, without worry of tripping over the canines.

Andrew shouted encouragement to Honey and moved aside to block Lyness Eastman from passing, but that left the way clear for Hartwell to charge forward and draw even with Josephine. He didn't pass her, keeping the two of them riding alongside each other for several lengths.

The baron and the duke's daughter were a well-matched pair in their riding. Both elegantly dressed, on horses that would cost hundreds of pounds if they went up for auction, and laughing as they rode.

This was who Simon wanted for his sister.

Lord Hartwell and Lady Josephine, wedded. Living far away, in York, where she would be mistress of the barony's home and heart.

Andrew's stomach dropped, and the world went quiet. A rushing filled his ears. A frown curled his lips. And the warm spring day turned gray and cold.

Honey stumbled, hitting a rut that nearly sent both of them to the ground. Andrew shifted, guided her to more even ground, and slowed to let her regain her footing. Her balance returned, her stride lengthened, and Andrew looked up again to see four riders ahead of him, and the agreed-upon finish line in sight.

He'd lost the race.

But the knowledge he must serve the others tea while wearing an apron, frills or not, didn't disturb him. No. But the feeling that he was soon to lose something far more precious had touched his heart. Dread had clutched at that vital organ as he finally gained the end of the course, and it took some time for him to breathe easily once more.

He endured the jests at his expense, wearing a good-humored mask, and let the rest of the party return ahead of him with the excuse that he must see to his horse after her stumble. Ensuring she had suffered no injury.

The men started up the path to the castle, but Josephine, her cheeks pinked by the exercise and her shoulders relaxed, didn't follow right away. She came to stand beside him, her hand on Honey's nose.

"Poor girl. You do not think she did herself a serious injury, do you?" she asked, not looking at Andrew, and missing the way he stared at her. The moment he realized he was studying her profile, the curve of her nose, the way her lips parted as she murmured to the horse, he yanked himself a step away. Shook his head. Forced a laugh.

"No, of course not. She put a foot wrong is all. The stable master will have her set to rights if there's so much as a hair out of place." He took the lead and stepped away. "Come, Honey."

Josephine lowered her hand as the horse turned away, and from the corner of his eye, he caught the startled expression on her face. "Andrew. You aren't upset about losing the wager, are you?"

"No." He forced a laugh. He needed to get away from her before he said something foolish. His composure had slipped, and

Josephine couldn't see—she knew him too well. Letting her guess at his thoughts would prove disastrous. "May I depend on you to procure my apron? I think a maid might have an easier time handing one over to you than to me." He didn't meet her gaze. Not quite.

There was a too-long measure of silence before she answered. "Of course." She took a step closer, and his gaze flicked to hers and away, but not before he saw the concern in them. "Andrew? Is something—"

A large dog appeared at her side and barked. Whether it was Athena or Apollo, Andrew didn't know, but the beast drew Josephine's attention away, and he made his escape into the stables.

By the time he and the stable master finished their conversation about Honey's care, Josephine and the others were long gone. Leaving Andrew to walk up to the castle alone.

"What is wrong with me?" he muttered to the gravel path. He took off his hat as he trudged upward and found a handkerchief to wipe his brow. He wasn't overly hot. Not dizzy. Nor did he have an upset stomach. Yet despite all of that, he felt distinctly ill.

And it had started the moment he'd thought of Josephine going away.

The moment he'd thought of her leaving, with Hartwell, to live in faraway York.

What business was it of his where she lived? She must, eventually, leave Clairvoir. And her family. That meant leaving him behind too, of course. That was the nature of things.

But things had been *odd* between them lately.

Ever since they'd left London, he'd felt a change in his regard for Josephine. A change he'd tried desperately to ignore. First, there had been the realization that he wondered what it would be like to kiss her.

That had to be a natural inclination any man would feel when faced with a beautiful woman. He'd never denied Josephine's good looks, to himself or anyone else. A man would have to be blind to think her anything other than attractive.

Not that he went around thinking of kissing every pretty woman. That would make him a cad.

But then. Why Josephine?

"Opportunity," he said to himself. "That's all." He was around her more than any woman of his acquaintance. Again, that was completely natural, given his friendship with her brother and his place in the duke's family.

The thought of kissing aside, he'd also found himself more sympathetic to her than in the past. More aware of her comings and goings, which had led him to following her to the village. Then up to her tower.

*But it is my duty to look after her, since I promised her father and Simon both I would be of help while the duke is in London.* He nodded along with that thought. *I am completely justified in my concern for her.*

It all made perfect sense when he looked at the course of events that had led him to spending more time in Josephine's company. No wonder his instincts had shifted. He was merely following a natural course that had brought them closer, as friends.

As Josephine's friend, and Simon's, too, he would concern himself over her future. He must naturally mourn the thought of losing her, even if it was to one as worthy as Roman Eastman, Lord Hartwell.

"Yes, of course." He lifted his gaze upward as he stepped from beneath the last canopy of trees and into the terraced gardens nearest the hilltop and castle. "She is my friend."

His friend, Josephine. His friend, who had felt comfortable in his arms while they rode in the rain. A necessary thing, that ride, to get them out of the weather. It wasn't his fault they'd only had the single horse. Josephine. His friend, whose laugh made his heart lighter, and whose lips made him think of soft kisses in the cool shadows of the woods.

Andrew stopped where he stood and gulped.

*No. I cannot entertain such thoughts about Josephine. She is Simon's sister. The duke's daughter. We are, and only will be, friends.*

Until someone like Hartwell took her away to wed.

Andrew's heart cracked, and the sick feeling returned. He replaced his hat, then rubbed at his chest above the ache he hadn't realized was there.

"Perhaps I am a fool," he whispered, and the breeze snatched his words away before he could take them back.

# CHAPTER 15

The day after their ride, and the enjoyable sight of Andrew serving everyone tea while wearing a white-frilled apron, Josephine slipped away again. She climbed the steps to her secret nest in the tower, holding a bundle of paper against her chest. It was fresh, in large sheets, and would need to be cut down to the right size. A chore she didn't at all mind performing herself in the quiet of her hideout.

But as soon as her eye level rose above the final step, she paused and put her free hand against the wall to catch her balance.

Andrew already sat in her tower, in the same place as he had before. Instead of reading, he leaned back against the corner of the wall and window, staring out the slightly open glass frame. He didn't wear his coat. Which she didn't blame him for, as the afternoon had turned somewhat warm for spring. His blond curls fell over his brow and across his ears. As she stood there, still on the steps and mostly in shadow, she watched as his chest rose and fell with a large breath. Then he closed his eyes and leaned his head back against the stone.

If only she could linger there on the step, absorbing the peace of the scene. Having Andrew there, in her sanctuary, didn't irritate her as she thought it should. Instead, his presence complimented the atmosphere. He belonged there, at least as much as she did. And oh, how she wished she had the words to tell him that.

How could she call herself an author, or even a writer, when she couldn't speak her heart to someone she had known nearly her entire life?

Andrew rubbed at a spot on his forehead before releasing a sigh, still ignorant of her arrival.

He seemed weary, but why? No one was as invigorated by riding as Andrew. And why did she find herself wishing to smooth away the crease of worry in his forehead? She frowned and reminded herself that he was an interloper. An uninvited guest. She needn't waste any time or thought on worrying after his comfort.

She took another step, and then another, and finally the soft sound of her slipper on the stone was enough to stir him. She sent her icy glares at him as best she could, ignoring the way his crooked smile made her wish to smile back.

"What are you doing here?" Oh dear. She hadn't sounded nearly as affronted by his presence as she wished.

His smile transformed into a wide grin. "Good afternoon, Josie. I brought you pastries."

She blinked. "Pastries?"

"Of course. And I commandeered a tea tray for you." He made a flourishing gesture with his hand, and she spied a small tray with a teapot and two cups waiting for her in the middle of the floor.

"Oh."

"That is all you can say? 'Oh?' After I have risked life and limb to bring you all the comforts of home?" He sighed as though greatly put upon. "I suppose I could take it away again."

Despite her efforts, at his overly dismal tone, she laughed.

"Andrew, you ninny. I am delighted by the refreshments. Thank you for providing them." Rather than sit in her usual place, Josephine took the piece of carpet directly beside him, the better to nudge his shoulder with her own. "But I must confess myself to some disappointment."

Andrew's lips quirked upward as he poured tea from the little pot into a cup for her. "Do tell, my lady. It is my shame if I have given you any reason to be less than completely satisfied."

Josephine put the pile of paper at her side and accepted the cup from him. "It is a simple thing. Merely that you are not wearing the delightful apron from the last time you poured my tea."

Andrew tilted his head back and laughed, loudly enough to startle Josephine into nearly dropping her cup. Which only made him laugh more, and then she could not help joining in.

"It was a most fetching apron, wasn't it?" he said, his eyes still alight with mirth.

Josephine didn't dare take a sip of the tea yet, as the memory of Andrew's flounces as he poured tea for all those gathered made her snicker again. A most unladylike sound, her grandmother would say. "I cannot believe you were the one to wear it. I truly hoped it would've fallen to Simon."

"Alas, your brother proved a superior horseman yesterday." Andrew poured his own cup of tea and leaned back against the stone wall. His shirtsleeve brushed her skin at the elbow, making a prickle of awareness travel along her arm. But she didn't move.

It was only Andrew. They were alone. What did it matter?

She heaved a sigh of relief. "I didn't think I could slip away today. Not without Grandmama noticing."

"Your stealth impresses me." Andrew put his cup down and picked up a pastry. "You'd be a natural spy. You should inquire at the Home Office."

Josephine chuckled, then sighed. "Hand me one of those tarts, won't you?" He passed her an apple tart. She settled more comfortably against the wall, uncaring if she mussed her curls.

Andrew went back to his pastry, devouring it in two quick bites. He brushed his hand off on his trousers. "You avoided Hartwell rather neatly, too."

"Troublesome of him to want my attention, isn't it?" She tried to smile, but it felt weak. She wasn't one to speak unkindly of others, and this felt nearly the same. "I promised to show him the gardens this afternoon."

For a moment, she thought Andrew went stiff beside her. But then he moved to pick up the plate of pastries to offer her another of her choice. "I didn't think he was interested in horticulture."

"He isn't." Josephine picked up a bilberry tart next. "It is an excuse, I gather, to speak with me." She nibbled at the edge of the flaky crust. "These are delicious. How did you manage to get all of it up here?"

"That is my secret, I'm afraid." Andrew folded his arms and closed his eyes.

"I told you my secret," she reminded him.

He cracked open one eye to look down at her. "That doesn't mean I must now tell you mine, does it?" He closed his eye again. "I thought you didn't like it when your family played at matchmaking."

"I don't." Josephine took a larger bite of her treat, then chewed slowly. Hoping Andrew wouldn't press the subject. She had no such luck.

"Simon rarely takes part in such schemes, I thought."

"Almost never, beyond introducing me to his friends at social events." She focused on eating the last bite without dropping the dark purplish tart filling onto her gown. Then she brushed at the crumbs on her lap. "I have discussed the matter with him. He knows I am not happy about it."

"The idea of you and Hartwell. It's strange."

Josephine agreed with him. "I know. It isn't as though he has ever showed interest before."

"Nor you in him, I gather." Andrew had gone stiff beside her again.

"Never." She leaned a little closer to him, their arms flush from shoulder to elbow. The pleasant sensation of connection, brief as it was, seemed to make Andrew relax. She caught him smiling, though his eyes remained closed.

What was it her grandmother had said about Andrew? That he was jealous, independent, and needful. A strange combination of things. How could one be all three at the same time? And why?

She understood his desire for independence, as she felt it often enough herself. But needful? What could he need?

He was all alone in the world, except for her family and his cousin Emma. He didn't have anyone else that she knew of. Perhaps that explained both the needfulness and the jealousy.

"Andrew?"

"Hm?"

"Do you ever wish things were different?"

His eyebrows drew together but his eyes remained shut. "What things?"

Josephine plucked at the fabric of her gown, pinching and twisting it nervously. She gathered her words and spoke them with care. "Do you ever wish you had brothers and sisters, like I have?"

He shrugged, the loose cotton of his sleeve stroking her skin and making it prickle again. "Sometimes, I suppose. But then, that is one reason I am forever here at the castle. Your parents have been kind enough to make me feel like part of the family. Simon is like a brother to me. The girls are as dear to me as sisters. I would happily spend hours with James exploring the woods, too. He's a diverting little fellow."

Josephine watched him speak, tracing the line of his nose with her gaze, then studying his lips. Wondering. "What about me?"

"You?"

"Yes, me. You've said we are friends."

"Indeed."

"Do you consider me as a sister, like you do Isabelle and Rosalind?" She held her breath, her heart lifting hopefully, her mind so close to understanding something. *If* he gave the right answer.

First, he coughed covering his mouth with a fist, and turned away from her. Then the cough became a laugh, strained as it was. "You? A sister?" The scorn in his voice wounded her. Even though she'd wanted him to say no, she hadn't wanted him to say it like that. The tone of his answer squashed her confidence.

She forced herself to laugh. "I suppose not. We don't get on well at all, do we?" She picked up her pile of paper and moved to her usual place. "We are more like a cat and dog than a brother and sister."

Andrew had recovered. "We are getting on well at present."

"Out of necessity, I think. A sort of cease-fire." She picked up her writing desk. She did her best not to look at him. "I think I shall write until it's time to go to the garden." She waved toward the steps. "If you don't have a book today, you ought to leave so I can concentrate."

"I've been meaning to ask—what are your writing about?"

She hushed him, sending a burning glare in his direction. "None of your business. Off you go. I have work to do."

He hesitated, then gathered up the tea things. "Do you want this last pastry?"

She didn't even check what flavor it was. "No. Thank you."

"Josie." He sounded uncertain. Perhaps even a bit sorry. "I didn't mean to laugh like that."

She tightened her grip around her quill. "*Please*, Andrew. Not now. I haven't any time as it is, and I wish to write. We can talk again later."

Andrew hesitated only a moment more before he stood. "Of course. I apologize for bothering you. Happy writing."

She nodded dismissively, dipping her quill in ink and scratching out nonsense words across the page. Waiting for him to leave. Listening as his shoes scraped quietly against the steps as he descended to the tower entrance.

Then she sighed and dropped her quill, only to gasp and hurry to blot out the ink puddle she made in her haste. "Terrible. Horrible. Awful." She muttered each word with more fire, then put aside her work. Not the old manuscript that had been rejected for reasons she could not guess, but the new one. The book she had started after Andrew had discovered her secret.

A story about a man and woman who rather detested each other. Something she had written a single scene for, in Andrew's presence, to give vent to her frustration over his invasion of her special place. But the words had flowed easily in this story. A story less fraught with drama and moral lessons, and full of more ridiculous moments between the enemies.

She closed her eyes. "I didn't want him to think of me as a sister," she reminded herself. But she hadn't wanted him to laugh at her, either. Why had he laughed?

Best she put it all from her mind. Instead, she would work on her old manuscript. And, when the time came, slip down to the garden for her walk with Lord Hartwell.

Two hours later, Josephine had put aside the hurt from Andrew's laughter well enough to focus her thoughts and feelings elsewhere. Such as how much she missed Emma all the more when Lord Hartwell met her outside for their walk through the gardens.

Because even though she'd invited her sisters to stroll with them, they didn't bother to keep close. No, her sisters walked twenty paces ahead with their heads bent together in conversation.

Josephine had rather counted on them to stay back and admire the handsome baron. Their disinterest in ogling him came as a disconcerting surprise. Emma would have stayed by her side, she well knew.

Simon had influenced their behavior. There wasn't another explanation for it. They wouldn't miss an opportunity to giggle over an eligible gentleman unless their eldest brother, to whom both girls were excessively devoted, had directed them otherwise.

"Your family's home is incredible." Lord Hartwell walked beside her, hands clasped behind his back, as he took in the gardens and trees. "The lengths your mother went to in the castle's creation have become the stuff of legend in Society. Do you share her interest in architectural pursuits?"

It wasn't an uncommon question. She could answer easily and with a benign smile. "My mother ensured I studied the modern masters of that particular art, but no. I am not passionate about building plans, buttresses, and columns as she is."

"Understandable. My father's passions leaned toward astronomy and mathematics. It was something of a disappointment for him when neither of his sons showed a natural inclination for either beyond a routine knowledge of both." He bent to study the delicate purple buds in one of the flower beds. Keeping up the ruse, she supposed, that he had an interest in gardens.

"I suppose our parents hope to pass on to us the things they love. My mother has been content that we show an appreciation for the design and artfulness that goes into construction. My grandmother's fondness for gardens have likewise been passed to us, her grandchildren."

Lord Hartwell continued their walk at a slow pace, and Josephine counted herself lucky that he didn't mean to spend the whole of their time together flirting with her. Thus far, Hartwell hadn't paid her any extravagant compliments, or boasted of himself. Both things that previous would-be suitors had done ad nauseam.

"If not organizing building materials or gardens, my lady, what is it that you are most passionate about?"

Josephine's toe caught on the edge of an uneven stone, causing her a slight stumble—but Lord Hartwell's hand caught her elbow, steadying her. She swallowed back her embarrassment and smiled up at him. "Thank you."

He released her, his genial smile still in place, his light blue eyes kind. "I didn't realize my question would startle you. Forgive me."

Josephine laughed, the sound too airy. He *had* startled her and caused a misstep. "You take too much credit, sir. The uneven ground is to blame for that ungraceful moment. Not your question, which I can answer with ease." And falsehood. Because no one of her station could admit to writing for pleasure, unless they wrote poetry that Society would find acceptable enough to be read at dinner parties.

"Perhaps I am being unfair. Before I request that you reveal such things to me, I should tell you what I am most passionate about." He leaned toward her, though not inappropriately close, and whispered loudly, "I am devoted to the subjects of history and art."

That took her enough aback that her mouth popped open as she said, "Oh? Really?" She kept her pace beside him even when they began to walk once more, walking down a gentle slope to the next level of gardens.

"Quite. More so the appreciation of art, I will say. I cannot boast of being a talented painter. But I find myself excessively interested in historical research, and the paintings that allow us to see into the past."

"That is fascinating. I cannot say I know too many noblemen who would declare such a thing." She accepted his arm as he guided her down a set of stone steps into the statuary. "My father has an interest in history and the cultures of Europe." Doubtless, her father would enjoy long conversations about both with the baron. Another mark in his favor, she supposed.

And yet, despite their pleasant conversation, Josephine didn't feel any more inclined toward Roman Eastwood than she had the last time he'd visited the castle. Before he'd ever showed a modicum of interest in her. What *had* sparked his sudden interest? Besides her brother's invitation, of course.

Almost as though he heard her thoughts, Lord Hartwell paused where they stood. He regarded her seriously a moment, his hands tucked behind him once more.

Something in the solemnity of his gaze made her wish her sisters back. Or at least the dog. Anyone or anything that might keep him from saying whatever it was he prepared to say.

"I should like to come to know you better, Lady Josephine." He spoke her name with a preciseness and warmth that normally would put her on her guard. "Shall we be friends?" he asked, his eyes wrinkling at the corners with a teasing smile.

She stepped off the path and sniffed at a small pink bloom. What was she to say? Friendship was perfectly acceptable. He wasn't asking for a courtship. Not yet. And if she cut him off so early, when her whole family approved of him, would that be fair to him or anyone else? Though she hadn't any romantic inclination toward Hartwell, nothing about him repelled her, either.

She measured her words and adjusted her tone, trying to match his innocent request without giving too much encouragement. "I believe I can agree to a friendship, my lord."

"But only just." He chuckled and wisely moved to the other side of the path to examine the tree that hung above them. Had he approached her, or stood too close, she might have bounded away like a startled doe.

She turned to face him, the distance between them a relief. "What do you mean, Lord Hartwell?"

He looked down the path where her sisters had long since disappeared with his dogs, then tipped his head to the side as he regarded her closely. "You and I both know of the games people in Society play. I will be honest with you, my lady, if you are honest with me." He took a breath, and for the first time, the baron appeared uncertain. Even sheepish. "A friendship is all well and good, but if your affection is engaged elsewhere, and a friendship is all we will ever have, I would appreciate a forthright word on that account."

Heat blossomed in her chest and crept upward until she felt it in her cheeks. It was the first time he had pulled such a reaction from her. But it had nothing to do with him, and everything to do with someone who had laughed at her a short while before. "You wish to know if I have an understanding with someone?"

"No, my lady. I would not pry that far so soon." He brought his hands forward, then let them hang at his side, as though uncertain what to do with them. He made a fine picture in his vulnerability, which wasn't something she had seen much in the men of her acquaintance before. "I ask that if your heart is set on another, you tell me so I will not endanger my own as we come to know one another better. That is all."

It was the most honest thing a man with courtship in his mind had ever said to her. For a moment, she remembered standing in the rain with Andrew. When she had felt that strange reaction to him—warmth and a desire to step into his arms.

But that was hardly an engagement of her heart. Andrew would doubtless laugh if he knew, or guessed, at how often she had thought of that moment since its passing. Just as he had laughed at her in the tower.

The idea of Andrew laughing at her *again* made Josephine's answer obvious, even if it made her uneasy. "My heart is quite my own at present." Then she turned away, catching the way the baron's shoulders relaxed from the corner of her vision before she returned to the path. "We ought to find my sisters, my lord. They have quite made off with your dog."

She had no intention of discussing the matter further with

him. They had said enough for the present. He took the hint and offered his arm to escort her along the path.

Isabelle and Rosalind found them in the statuary. Upon seeing her master again, Athena trotted over rather more like a small pony than a dog. Her long, thin tail wagged happily as she sat at her master's feet, staring up at him with complete adoration. The dog's devotion to Lord Hartwell made the man somehow more endearing.

Did she have reason enough to entertain Lord Hartwell as a suitor? What would her father say about the matter, if he knew of her hesitation to declare her heart free? More so, what would he say if he knew she had entertained—even for a moment—the idea of a courtship with Sir Andrew?

# CHAPTER 16

With a small box in hand, Andrew sat in the window seat in his bedroom. He turned the box around and around, studying the dark-stained wood and delicate etching at its corners. Then he undid the latch, raising the lid on its delicate hinges, to reveal the pen inside. Pen and several steel nibs, each a different size, made to fit the pen and write better than a quill. Smoother.

Imagine. No more cutting quills to the right size. No more repairing the pens with a blade. No more tucking one feather's end into another to create a well of ink within the instrument itself.

Josephine would love it. She had stood there, with him, looking at this very pen through the window that day at the Burlington Arcade. He'd bought it for her the moment she left for home, her guard with her. He hadn't even hesitated to think why he wanted to give her the gift.

Then they'd left London. And the idea of presenting her with the pen was more than silly. It was discomfiting. How would he explain the gift? He hadn't made it a habit to buy her or anyone in the family presents before.

An impulsive buy had left him perplexed with his own

actions. Confused, even. And the more time he spent with Josephine, the worse it became.

He closed the lid with a snap and shoved a hand through his hair, tugging at it with frustration. What was wrong with him?

Rain pattered on the window. A common enough occurrence in spring. But it made him wish he was in the tower, reading a book, with Josephine working silently nearby.

When Josephine asked if he thought of her as a sister, he'd laughed at just how *wrong* that idea had struck him. Sister? No. Never. Not even when she was younger, and he tormented her with his jests and teased her to distraction. It had been childish of him, of course. But of late...he teased to make her laugh. To see her smile. To watch as she would shake her head at him, purse her lips, all while her eyes twinkled with amusement.

He'd been her jester. Her fool. Delighting in every smile, every laugh, and every time she joined him in his tomfoolery. And neither of them had known it.

He'd enjoyed their ceasefire, too. If that was all it was to her, it didn't matter. For him, passing time in her company in peace had meant something else. Something more.

But with one ill-timed laugh, one startled reaction, he had offended her. Perhaps setting them back to where their relationship had been in London. Before the play. Before the Arcade. Back to the years and years of banter and badgering.

Which wouldn't do. Not if he wanted to explore these new thoughts and feelings. But how could he explain himself? Or repair the damage?

Especially with Hartwell dancing attendance on Josephine.

Putting aside the box, Andrew rose to his feet and pulled on his coat. He'd left the one he'd worn all day in the tower, having forgotten it in his haste to withdraw from Josephine and get his mind straight.

It was nearly dinner time, and he was no closer to tidying the mess of his thoughts than he had been hours before. Perhaps he would find Simon. Or even Hartwell. Someone to talk to of hunting or fishing, or tenants and taxes. Anything would be better than being alone with his thoughts of Josephine.

As he turned at the corridor's end to come to the staircase, he paused. The dowager duchess stood at the top of the steps speaking with Sterling. The guard, dressed as a servant, appeared as stoic as ever.

"Yes, Your Grace," Sterling was saying as Andrew approached. "But if you wish for a more detailed report, you must speak with the lieutenant."

"Your assurance is good enough." She waved away his suggestion, then saw Andrew. "Ah. And here is our baronet. What do you think, Sir Andrew? Sterling here assures me that we are all perfectly safe. Not so much as a scent of discontent on the castle grounds."

"The duke has always cared for his people. They know that, and whatever the problems in London, they will not follow his family here." Andrew nodded to Sterling, who bowed in return. "Have you reason for your concern, Your Grace?"

"A letter from my son. Someone threw a stone at the duchess's carriage." She shivered. "Cecilia is unharmed, of course. Though I imagine she wasn't pleased. But what if the fool who threw it had hit a horse, sending them dashing into danger? Or broken a window?"

Andrew silently offered the woman his arm, which she took with a perfunctory nod of her head. He did not think he imagined the way she briefly leaned against him before pulling herself aright. Worry deepened the wrinkles around her eyes and mouth. The dowager duchess, a dragon in many respects, had a soft heart when it came to her family.

He didn't like seeing her worry.

"The duchess is unharmed, Your Grace. I am certain the duke will take all the necessary precautions to keep her and himself that way. Just as Simon does here at the castle to keep you and the other ladies protected." He led her down the steps at a pace which would allow her to maintain the elegant lift to her chin.

"Young man, you needn't indulge my worrying, nor condescend to offer me platitudes and reassurances. I am nearly eighty years old." She sniffed. "The risks my son takes with his safety are quite apparent to me. But let us talk no more of such things so near dinner. I have no wish to ruin either of our appetites."

"I am yours to command." Andrew changed his tone to something lighter and merrier. "What would you like to speak about instead? I am well-versed on the weather, and matters pertaining to horses and stables. I can also speak at length on topics such as literature and art."

"I have heard your silver tongue speak on all of those things before, you incorrigible boy," she told him, though he caught the upward tilt to her mouth that reminded him of Josephine when she fought back a smile. "Let us try a new topic. What think you of Lord Hartwell?"

Unprepared for that question, Andrew blurted the first thing that came to mind. "I always liked him at school. And since then, I suppose." Though the baron's sudden appearance to court Josephine hadn't set well with him, and now he knew why. He stifled the urge to admit he'd like the baron to pack up and leave. Hartwell had no business swooping in to court Josephine. Not when Andrew was still putting the pieces of his own feelings together. "He is a fine chap."

"Fine enough for our Josie?" The dowager duchess tilted her head and her gray eyebrows rose high on her lined forehead. "None of us are ignorant of his purpose here, Andrew."

It wasn't a slight when she left off the "sir" before his name. It was her own way to make him feel a part of the family, even if she referred to her own male relatives by title rather than their Christian name. This time, when she spoke his name, there was an emphasis to it he didn't understand. It was almost a command. But what did she wish him to do?

"I suppose not," he muttered. They left the stairs and walked down the corridor to the room adjacent the less formal dining room. Not the large one where the duke held his grand dinners and invited guests, but the smaller, more intimate dining room on the floor beneath that one.

The family matriarch paused, pulling Andrew to a stop as well. They were in front of a very large painting that depicted the goddess of spring dancing in a grove of trees with her minstrels. Andrew took in the familiar painting, his thoughts unfocused.

"My granddaughter's birthday is the day after tomorrow," the dowager duchess said, breaking into his thoughts.

"I know," Andrew said absently.

The duchess released an exasperated puff of air. "We ought to do something to celebrate. Especially since her parents are not here."

"Yes, Your Grace." Andrew realized after a moment that Josephine's grandmother was glaring at him. He turned to her and offered an apologetic smile. "What did you have in mind?"

Her nose wrinkled at him, and she shook her head. "Never mind." She released his arm and went to the door, which a footman held open for her. Andrew was fairly certain he heard her mutter, "I thought he was an intelligent boy."

Andrew stared after her a moment, then sighed and pretended to look at the painting again. Josephine's birthday. Of course he knew it was approaching. Usually, once the upper classes left the schoolroom, their birthdays passed quietly. A favorite meal might be served. Flowers may appear in their rooms. Most considered celebration beyond that as excessive.

Except the duke gifted his wife something thoughtful on the anniversary of her birth, their marriage, and several other times throughout the year. He showered his wife with tokens, small and large, of his affection. He gave his children something to mark their birthdays, too. Even Simon had received his infamous walking stick as a gift from his father.

Lovers often gave one another tokens on such dates, too.

Andrew grimaced. Giving Josephine a gift on her birthday would be tantamount to declaring something he didn't think he could declare.

"Did Persephone offend you?" Josephine appeared at his side, staring up at the painting. She seemed pale. The look in her eyes somewhat distant. He had hurt her in the tower that morning. Because he could not say she was as a sister to him.

Was that really all she wanted? A siblings' relationship? His stomach turned over at the very idea. No. That would never be. She didn't look at him, so he turned his attention back to the dancing goddess.

He kept his voice light. "Yes. She offends me terribly."

"Really? I always liked her. What has she done to merit your enmity?" Josephine's tone was cautious. Perhaps she had grown as lost as he in their relationship. What had once been easy, the teasing and banter, now felt contrived.

Andrew took stock of the painting. "Her lack of shoes."

That startled a smile from Josephine. She arched one eyebrow and turned to Andrew with a quizzical smile. "Lack of shoes?"

Her smile was worth the ridiculous conversation. "Precisely. Look. Even the minstrels are wearing sandals, and she dances about as though spring isn't a time of thistles and thorns."

"I think the goddess of spring might be immune to such things." Josephine looked at the painting again. "And even if she wasn't, running about without shoes or stockings is delightful. I wish her well in the effort."

"You would." He chuckled as a memory came to him of a bright spring day from years' past. "How old were you when Simon and I caught you walking along the fountain edge without your shoes? It wasn't too long ago."

Her cheeks pinked, and she wrinkled her nose at him, the look similar to her grandmother's. "I was fourteen. And a lady can remove her shoes in her family's garden if she wishes."

"Ought she to hurl those shoes at young gentlemen, though?" he asked, narrowing his eyes and tapping his chin in thought. "I'm not certain what Society would think of that behavior."

"If the *boy* deserved it, then yes. Throwing shoes at irritating youths is perfectly acceptable." She sniffed and turned her nose up. "Especially when he implies the young lady has large feet."

"I didn't say that, surely." He chuckled, admiring her profile while wearing a mask of amusement.

"I remember precisely what you said." She turned toward him, and he mirrored the movement so they stood face to face with less than an arm's length between them. "You saw me walking along the edge of the fountain, bare footed. Simon asked if I had any trouble balancing on the narrow stone. Before I could answer, you said, 'Of course not. People with large feet always have good balance.'"

Andrew grinned, though the tips of his ears felt warm. He'd been a rascal. "I was an insufferable brat."

"I hated my feet for weeks after that," she scolded. "I wanted to strangle you with the laces of my slippers."

He stepped back, slowly, and looked down at the slippers she wore right then. They were a pale blue, the same color as her gown. "I'm not sure what I was thinking. Your feet seem perfectly sized now. Perhaps you grew into them."

She cast her eyes upward as though pleading with the heavens to strike him down, and then she met his gaze, a smirk tilting her pretty lips upward. "My aim has improved, Andrew. Do not tempt me into throwing these at you. I'm rather fond of them."

He raised both hands as though to surrender. "Peace, Josie. We're at a ceasefire, remember?"

Her amusement melted into an expression akin to disappointment. "I remember." She adjusted one of her gloves. "I am going to wait for the others. It is nearly dinner time."

Rather than let her leave him there, the air between them

SALLY BRITTON

heavy with uncertainty, Andrew offered his arm. "May I take you in to dinner tonight?"

A brief hesitation, then she took his arm. "Of course. But you needn't ask. Hartwell must take Grandmother in, and Simon cannot escort his sister, so it falls to you quite naturally."

They walked to the door, and the footman opened it for them.

"I know. It usually does." That was almost always how it fell. He would escort her in, or sit by her side, at family dinners and during more formal occasions. Then they would entertain themselves by debating the ridiculous, pretending to disagree merely to ruffle each other's feathers. He leaned closer just before parting with her at her favored chair to murmur, "But this time, I wanted you to know that I am glad for it."

She stared at him, her blue eyes wide, and he bowed before taking himself off to the other side of the room, leaving her to speak with her grandmother until the others arrived, one by one, for the evening meal.

HARTWELL SAT ACROSS THE TABLE FROM JOSEPHINE, AND Andrew sat at her side. Grandmother had relented to Simon's request and took one end of the table while he filled the other. Lyness sat on Josephine's other side, while her sisters flanked Lord Hartwell. The servants had removed several of the table leaves to make it smaller and more intimate for the eight of them.

Having her parents' chairs occupied was only marginally better than seeing them empty. Of course, the duke and duchess had left the family to travel together before. On those occasions, Josephine had missed them terribly but kept perfectly cheerful with the knowledge they were on an adventure. This was different, though.

She missed her mother. Her father. Emma. The people she

confided in were gone, leaving her to sort out her own thoughts and feelings.

Simon and Hartwell were speaking of York's citizenry, comparing the disquiet to what Simon had seen in London. The whole of it was most depressing. Especially given how little they could do to help.

"Your father has my admiration, fighting as he does for reform. I am surprised any radical would attack his carriage, given his stance on the Corn Laws as well as representation of the masses." Lord Hartwell paused in the conversation to serve one of Josie's sisters from the platter of fish before him, a perfect gentleman.

"Likely they do not recognize the heraldry of one nobleman over another," said the dowager duchess with a sniff.

"That is possible, I suppose." Simon leaned against the back of his chair and joined his hands together in front of him. "At least London isn't seeing the level of unrest I hear of in other parts of the country. Do you know that in Manchester and Birmingham there have been meetings held in parks where those in favor of the more radical reforms speak to the masses?"

"I understand in January there were more than ten thousand souls gathered to listen to that man—Henry Hunt, is his name—while the calvary watched from the sidelines."

"My father tells of another meeting in March, and says he expects one this month as well." Simon's expression darkened, and he looked down at his clasped hands. "Parliament has sent letters to the Lancashire magistrates, warning that they need to peacefully disperse such assemblies before they grow uncontrollable."

"People have the right to gather and listen to speakers, do they not?" Josephine asked, delicately poking at her fish with her fork.

"Of course they do," Simon answered. "At least at present. There were those laws in place, for a time, that prohibited large gatherings unless the magistrates agreed to them and attended. Father said there is talk of reinstating those laws, at least until things calm down."

Andrew spoke quietly from beside her, not looking up from the glass of wine in his hand. "The people are hungry, poor, and many are without work. So long as the government dissatisfies them, doing nothing to help them, they will keep meeting. In large groups or small. I fear it will come to violence before long."

"As does the duke," Simon said, voice low and eyes dark with worry. "Especially if men such as Henry Hunt keep drawing large, angry crowds."

Silence hung over the table, and Josephine didn't miss the worried looks exchanged by Isabelle and Rosalind. They were too young, surely, to hear such talk. But then, there were people even younger than them in the workhouses and fields, starving while the duke's daughters ate at a well-laden table.

Josephine's appetite diminished, and she lowered her fork.

Grandmama huffed, dabbing at her lips with a napkin. "Must we really speak of politics over dinner, my lords?" the dowager asked, weariness in her tone.

Josephine sent her grandmother a grateful smile. "I agree with Grandmama. Let us speak of pleasanter things." When she could do nothing to aid her countrymen but pray, she needed lighter fare at dinner.

"Such as your birthday?" Simon surprised her with the question. His hands unclasped, and he took up his cup, holding it as though to offer her a toast. "Father instructed me via letter to not let the day pass unmarked."

Lord Hartwell's eyebrows went up. "When is your birthday, my lady?"

"The day after tomorrow," Rosalind said, beaming up at him. "We always celebrate our birthdays."

Warmth flooded Josephine's cheeks. Birthdays were for children. When Lyness exchanged a grin with his brother, she hastened to say, "No one need worry over it. I haven't given it any thought."

"But the duke declares we must celebrate," Simon said,

sounding far too pleased with himself for having that argument ready. "You wouldn't have me ignore our father's orders, would you?"

The heat in her cheeks increased. "I really wish you wouldn't trouble yourselves, or the staff."

"What year do you mark, my lady?" Lyness asked.

His brother immediately shook his head, disapproval in his tone as he said, "You never ask that of a lady in company, Lyness."

"What company? It is only us and her family." Lyness didn't seem the least repentant.

They would not let the subject drop, Josephine well knew, until they were satisfied. She forced herself to smile. "I shall turn twenty."

"We usually have a special dinner." Isabelle volunteered the information with a gleeful expression. At nearly fifteen, she was old enough to behave more circumspectly. But with Lyness and Lord Hartwell at the table, she'd lost some of her good sense. "And Father always presents a gift. Did he send something for her, Simon?"

"He did." Simon's grin broadened. "I thought we might have a small party. Of course, most of our friends are still in London, but we have a few neighbors present who would be delighted to receive an invitation."

A party. Invitations. And Hartwell in residence intent on courting her. It all sounded rather awful at that moment. As much as she enjoyed hostessing dinners and parties with her mother, celebrating her birthday on such a scale without her parents present felt wrong. And foolish. "I would rather not worry about it," Josephine said, trying not to plead with her brother.

Simon was shaking his head, ready to insist. Lyness and Hartwell appeared equally enthusiastic about the idea, and her sisters were casting excited glances at one another. Grandmama had gone silent, though Josephine looked to her in hopes of finding an ally.

"I have an idea." Andrew's sudden statement brought the rest of the conversation to a stop. And, without meaning too, Josephine looked to the man at her right hand with hope. Even if he had been a principal tormenter in her past, he had been a friend of late. Understanding and even kind.

He met her gaze steadily, and the reassurance in his dark brown eyes soothed her frantic thoughts.

"Why don't I host a small gathering at my estate? Nothing grand. Perhaps a picnic on the grounds." He kept her gaze as he spoke, raising his eyebrows as he sought her approval of the scheme. It was a good plan. It took away the hosting duties from the family, and a picnic was informal enough that she needn't feel her parents' absence too keenly. Nor would a picnic allow Simon to make a spectacle of her.

Josephine gave the barest nod of approval, and Andrew turned to the others with a wide smile in place.

"It has been ages since I have hosted anything at Bytham. We can get there in two hours by carriage at an easy pace—the roads are well-maintained. I'll go ahead to make preparations, and Josephine may invite whomever she wishes."

The tightness in her chest eased. "That sounds like the perfect way to spend a birthday. I do enjoy picnics." She looked to Simon, who appeared to mull the idea over. "Come, Simon. Father won't mind if we visit Bytham Castle." They would doubtless bring several of the guards, making the venture safe.

She drew her sisters in to the idea. "You may both come, of course. Since it will be a small, informal gathering of friends, so long as your governess accompanies you, there is nothing wrong with the two of you joining us."

"Really? May we, Grandmama?" Rosalind, only thirteen years old and far from being out in Society, pled with wide eyes and hands pressed together as if in supplication.

"I suppose that would not cause too much of a social uproar,"

Grandmama said with dry amusement. "Will there be a provision for children at this picnic of yours, Sir Andrew?"

"Absolutely, Your Grace. And will you join us, too?" he asked with a differential tone.

"I think so. A little sunshine would be lovely. If the weather holds." She gestured for the servants to bring forward the last course of the evening. "I think we must agree to the picnic, Farleigh."

Simon smirked and nodded his ascent, and Josephine wanted to melt into a puddle of relief. She gave Andrew a grateful smile, then sat forward again. Her gaze collided with Lord Hartwell's.

He stared at her, his brow furrowed and a contemplative tilt to his head. His blue eyes flicked from her to Andrew at her side, then he raised his eyebrows at her and his expression smoothed over, relaxed and pleasant once more. He raised his cup to her. "I look forward to marking the anniversary of your birth, my lady."

"Thank you, Lord Hartwell." She lifted her own cup and sipped delicately from it.

She would have to find a way to thank Andrew for his picnic idea later. Despite the odd change in their relationship, he had shown himself a friend. Though contenting herself with that alone made her heart twist miserably, Josephine had to admit herself grateful for that much.

Somehow, she had to overcome her growing feelings for her brother's best friend. Perhaps he didn't care for her as she had begun to care for him. He might always see her as the little girl who argued with him over ridiculous things. And she had to content herself with that and nothing more.

# CHAPTER 17

A picnic at Bytham. What had he been thinking?

The morning after he proposed the idea, Andrew set off for his estate. Riding Honey, and leaving his protesting valet behind, Andrew could be there in far less time than it would take a carriage. And he would need every minute of that saved time to get things in order for Josephine's picnic.

He'd wanted to do something for her. Especially when he'd watched her squirm beneath Simon's ideas for her birthday. Josephine had always been the consummate hostess, thanks to her mother's tutelage, but she never had enjoyed being the center of attention. Despite her position in Society, her public nature remained quiet.

As Honey took him through Clairvoir Vale and into the surrounding hills, the sun-dappled road shadowed and cool, Andrew questioned his sanity multiple times.

What had the others thought when he proposed the idea? The dowager duchess had taken his measure with a twinkle in her eye. After their strange conversation on the stairs, he couldn't help wondering if she might suspect something of his growing feelings for Josephine.

*Growing feelings.* He snorted, and Honey flicked her ear back at him and snorted back. He'd kept from thinking about his feelings for Josephine for some time. Hadn't admitted a thing about them, especially to himself.

The night before, when the ladies had excused themselves after dinner, Simon had given him an odd look as he said, "You needn't host a picnic for Josephine. We could have it here instead."

"I haven't had a guest, let alone a party of guests, to Bytham in ages." He had tried to sound relaxed. Unbothered. Almost bored. "It would be good for the staff, too. Put them on their mettle. In fact, plan for your family—Hartwell and Lyness, too—to stay the night. We can all attend Bytham's chapel on Sunday before you begin the return journey."

He didn't say more. He didn't explain the frenzied plans in his mind, nor what it would mean for him to see Josephine in Bytham. She hadn't visited in years. Maybe he needed to see her there, to imagine her in his world rather than he in hers, and then he would know. Then he could admit to—something more.

The road, well-tended and in fine form considering the spring rains, gave him the peace he needed to think and plan. It also gave him far too much time to recall some of his less flattering memories with Josephine. When he had nettled her, again and again, before his year-long trip to Ireland. He had left to accompany Simon while the duke's heir learned all he could of their far-flung estate.

And when he had come home, last year, and met Josephine again for the first time since leaving for Ireland—he had known, even then, that something had changed. But he'd ignored it for nigh-on a year. Ignored every pull toward her. He'd fought and debated with as much spirit as he had in the past. He'd teased, jested, and aggrieved her. All to avoid admitting to himself that things were different. That his feelings had changed.

Andrew crested the last hill and looked down into the village.

He took High Street through to Castlegate, bypassing the tall mound upon which the castle that had given the town its name had once stood, until it had burned to the ground during the war between the royal houses of York.

Sixty years before, the king had given Andrew's family the mound and the grounds surrounding it, and it was at the farthest reaches of those grounds that another castle stood. Smaller, and a castle more by its nature of stone than any sort of grandeur. It wasn't like Clairvoir Castle, rebuilt with a fortune and an eye for design.

He turned right down the nameless road that led to his family's home. A baronetcy wasn't much. And they hadn't held the title long. The Crown had created the title to go with the castle, which was really only a small stone edifice meant by King James to be a place of refuge for his spies and favored courtiers. Kept ready by the baronets.

Andrew passed beneath the heavy canopy of trees that secreted his home away from the world. His castle didn't stand on a hill. It was tucked away. Built of gray stone, it had a cellar, two floors, and attics. There were ten bedrooms, but none of them as large as Andrew's guest quarters at Clairvoir.

He dismounted his horse at the door at the same moment the butler, Sutton, flung it open in welcome.

"Welcome home, Sir Andrew," the butler, old enough to be Andrew's father, puffed his chest out and worked hard to conceal a genuine smile. "It is good to see you, sir."

"Thank you, Sutton. Though you may not feel that way for long." Andrew looked up at his house, counting the widened windows his father had put in decades before to make the inside of the house brighter. "Guests are coming close at my heels. They will be here tomorrow, in fact, before noon."

Rather than appear troubled, the butler followed Andrew inside with his usual vigor and good cheer. He helped Andrew remove his overcoat, hat, and gloves. Peter, a footman, appeared to take those things away.

"I will send for Mrs. Caswell," Sutton said. "I am certain the staff will have no trouble making ready for your guests, sir."

Andrew took in the smallish entry, so different from the long corridor arrayed with swords and shields, the guardroom with its giant fireplaces to welcome guests, that Clairvoir Castle boasted. His home was humble by comparison. Doors on either side of the entry led to the rooms of the house, which opened up into one another rather than having long passages to connect them.

The floors were highly polished stone on the ground level and wood above. The walls, ancient as they were, had been plastered over by one of his predecessors and hung with artwork by family members for generations. None of Vandyck's work here. No Dutch or Italian masterpieces adorned his halls.

He swallowed. His home wasn't opulent, and perhaps not even elegant by some standards. But it was comfortable, safe, and all he had to offer besides himself.

A joyful greeting burst from the housekeeper the moment she walked through the arched doorway that led to the rear of the house where the servants worked. "Sir Andrew, welcome home. We didn't know to expect you, sir, or we'd have turned out to greet you properly."

Though he didn't deserve their fondness, given his long absences, Andrew drank in the familiarity and warmth of his servants with gratitude. Whether or not they knew it, they would have a hand in his choice of their future mistress.

As Andrew walked through his house with his two most senior servants following behind, he gave them all the information he could about their coming guests and his hopes for their brief stay and entertainment. Though the size of his castle, his larder, and even his pocketbook should have dampened his spirits, Andrew could only think that a woman of Josephine's status would have to be quite special to accept him as a suitor.

If he could see Josephine in those rooms, walking through his modest gardens, then he would know—he felt certain of it— whether they could put down their barbed words and witty retorts long enough to fall in love.

"When did we last visit Sir Andrew's castle?" Rosalind asked in the carriage as they bumped along the road. She and Isabelle sat on either side of their governess while Mrs. Robinson read from a book.

"Four years ago." Josephine kept her eyes on the passing scenery. She and her grandmother had the forward-facing seat, and between them was a basket of gifts for Andrew's home. "You were little more than an infant," she added with a teasing smile.

"Nine years old is not an infant." Rosalind sniffed and folded her hands in her lap, lifting her chin higher still. "You were only sixteen. Not out of the schoolroom."

"Children." Grandmama eyed them both with displeasure. "When you are as old as I am, you will realize that anyone under forty ought to be considered a juvenile, and under twenty an infant. You have no scope of the world just yet, for all you think yourselves so wise."

Mrs. Robinson brought her book a little higher to hide her knowing smile, and Josephine bit her lip to keep from giggling at Rosalind's affronted expression. Both granddaughters dutifully chorused, "Yes, Grandmama," as they ought before Isabelle changed the subject.

"Why do so many guards come with us?" She motioned upward to the top of the carriage. Their driver was a coachman, of course, but one of their father's specially trained men rode beside him and another on the back of the carriage. There was yet another riding on one of the horses pulling the vehicle, then a fourth on his own mount.

"Because Simon knows that is how Father would want it." Josephine looked out the window once more. "Even if we are unlikely to be set upon by thieves or radicals, more sets of eyes and ears make us doubly safe."

"It seems like an awful lot of fuss," Rosalind said, leaning against the window. "I wish we were still in London, or that Mother and Father were here with us."

"So do we all, dear child." The dowager duchess's eyes softened. "Parliament cannot hold the session forever. In the meantime, we must enjoy our spring and summer as best we can."

More people had fled London, thanks to the progressively larger crowds appearing at corners and parks to listen as orators decried the economy and political situation. Which meant Josephine had managed to invite two other families, friends of theirs, to join them for a day of picnicking and games at Sir Andrew's home.

Mr. and Mrs. Josiah Hepsworth, a family of large fortune, had agreed to come with their daughters, Maria (newly engaged, so that ought to keep her from pestering Simon), Hannah, and fifteen-year-old Elspeth, a friend to Isabelle and Rosalind.

Simon had invited the rector, who borrowed one of the duke's horses, as he kept none of his own. And Andrew had hinted that he would invite a family or two from Bytham's village.

Josephine startled when a rider appeared outside her window, jostling her from her thoughts. The road's width hadn't allowed her brother or his friends to ride parallel to the carriage for most of the journey. But there Lord Hartwell was, atop his dappled-gray steed, cutting an attractive figure as he rode.

He turned to look into the carriage and spied Josephine. He grinned and tipped his head to her, which she returned with a smile and nod of her own. Then he continued forward, moving ahead of the carriage.

Despite her agreement to explore a friendship with the man, Josephine heartily wished him elsewhere. Not with any malice, of course. But she remembered well that Andrew's castle was smaller than her own, which meant close quarters with all the guests when they were not picnicking out of doors.

With Hartwell on one side and Andrew on the other, Josephine imagined feeling rather squeezed between them. A new "friend," with hopes for more, and an old enemy, growing dearer to her with each passing day, would doubtless send her already complicated thoughts into a muddle.

Josephine hadn't planned on entering any romantic entanglements this year. Or the next. But perhaps one couldn't plan for such things. And once they came, everything moved quickly. Too quickly to wrap one's mind around the situation to make clever choices.

To so many of her acquaintances, ladies coming out into Society with wealth and beauty backing them, love had been a game.

But for Josephine, it was everything. And if love was within her grasp, did she dare to reach for it?

When the carriage came to a stop before the near-hidden castle, Josephine peered out at the gray-stone building that was more house than fortress. She saw Andrew, dressed in a dark blue coat and tall riding boots, ready for his guests and grinning infectiously.

It was Andrew who opened the carriage door to assist first the dowager duchess to step down. Then his hand returned to take Josephine's, and she saw the forget-me-not blue of his waistcoat, which matched the color of her gown so perfectly it looked as though they had planned it.

Did she imagine the gentle squeeze to her hand as Andrew murmured, "Welcome to my home, Lady Josephine."

Then he released her to help the governess and her sisters alight from the carriage, too, and Josephine looked up at the castle. There was a tower at one corner that likely allowed anyone inside to look over the tree-tops to the road.

The small castle, surrounded by trees filled with birdsong, brought back the memories of her last visit. The memories of walking through quiet, comfortable rooms where she felt she could tuck herself into a chair or window seat and read for hours. She remembered sitting beneath the trees and sketching with Emma while they talked of nothing.

Despite the sounds of people, horses, and carriages surrounding her now, the memory of that peace touched her heart once more. She relaxed. Then grinned.

Andrew led them into the castle, giving everyone time to freshen up before they continued through to the gardens. Josephine was among the first to step out into the sunshine once more, though the cool shadows of the castle beckoned her to stay and rest. Andrew waited on the terrace, looking through the hedges. He stood with a straight back, his hands clasped behind him, staring out over the maintained lawn of green stretching into a meadow and the stream just out of sight.

Josephine approached him, coming to his side and tucking her hands behind her back, too. "Your home is welcoming."

He glanced at her from the corner of his eye, and his smile grew softer. "Do you think so? I have always liked it, though there is much room for improvement. As your mother so often reminds me."

"Mother loves her building projects." Josephine arched an eyebrow at him. "You seemed quite keen last time she spoke of enlarging your castle with a new wing."

"If it would improve things." He shrugged. "But I don't suppose I will make changes anytime soon. The future lady of my castle will likely have her own ideas of how things should be."

Her heart stuttered, the warmth in her breast flickering like a candle, when he mentioned his nonexistent wife. Had she become enough enamored of him that she pictured herself in that role so soon?

The butler approached Andrew, bowing, and the baronet

excused himself a moment. Josephine watched him re-enter the castle, wondering at the change that had come over him in his own home. Andrew had always struck her as confident, but here was a new sort of self-possession, a maturity she rarely glimpsed, as he behaved as the master of his home.

Grandmama emerged onto the terrace in time to catch Josephine's stare, and she raised her eyebrows at her grand-daughter as she approached. "You seem happy, Josephine."

"I am quite content." Josephine looped her arm through her grandmother's. "Shall we stroll through the wildflowers?" When the dowager duchess agreed, Josephine led them down the steps and into the wilds of Sir Andrew's gardens.

# CHAPTER 18

Gathered beneath the shade of a willow, near the rapidly moving stream that bisected the baronet's property, Andrew's guests enjoyed a fine repast. Cold ham, rolls, slices of decadent cheese, preserves made from last summer's berries, cherry wine, and pastries fresh from the village bakery.

The cook hadn't been best-pleased with the idea of a party descending on him without notice, despite the fact that most would be leaving after the picnic for their own homes. Mrs. Caswell had cleverly suggested the bakery as a way to supplement the meals from their own unready larder.

Sutton had directed the preparations with his usual good cheer, and they had made the rest of the house ready with the aid of villagers eager to put extra coin in their purses. Andrew wasn't in residence often, and with only one man to wait upon, the castle hadn't had a full staff in years.

"A charming way to spend an afternoon, Sir Andrew, I must say." Mrs. Hepsworth spoke with her usual tone of self-importance and bluster. "The invitation delighted us, did it not?" She turned to her daughters, arrayed on the rug around her, along with Isabelle and Rosalind.

Andrew tried to show attention to all his guests while keeping an eye on Josephine. She sat on a rug, a cushion beneath her, with her grandmother on one side and Lord Hartwell on the other. He could've done without Hartwell's nearness, but Andrew satisfied himself that Josephine smiled as bright as the spring sunshine.

"I am pleased you could come, Mrs. Hepsworth." Andrew bowed at the waist, prepared to move on, when Miss Hannah waved her dainty hand at him.

"Oh, Sir Andrew," she half-whispered to him. "Do tell us more about your other guests. We have never met Lord Hartwell or his brother until today. Do you know them well?" Her eyes cut to the others.

Andrew crouched down to bring him into an easier speaking distance with the young woman, whose admiration of the baron wasn't at all surprising. The Hepsworth ladies had always set their sights on highborn men. "Hartwell is an old school chum. Farleigh and I have known him for years. His brother is a few years younger."

"How very interesting. And they reside in York?"

"Most of the time, yes. Indeed, they prefer York to London." If Andrew expected that to mark the other men with disfavor for the young women, he saw at once that it didn't dissuade them at all.

"A baron," Miss Hepsworth, the betrothed sister, said with a gleeful wave of her fan. "Think on it, Hannah."

The youngest Hepsworth sister, Elspeth, actually met Andrew's eyes and winced. She mouthed the word, "Sorry," and Andrew's estimation of Isabelle and Rosalind's young friend went upward. He rose and went next to the gathering of chairs beside the stream where the rector, Mr. Wood, spoke with Andrew's invited neighbors.

The Pratts had brought their children—little boys who had taken one look at Hartwell's massive dogs and fallen in love with the beasts. Hartwell had readily given the boys permission to play with the dogs, though Lyness had followed after the enthusiastic children and animals, doubtless to keep watch.

Simon shifted from group to group like Andrew, speaking with everyone, as the duke would if he were present. The duke's heir never really took a day away from his responsibilities, present or future. It was something Andrew had noticed years before, and the reason why he tried to involve Simon in as much of his mischief as possible.

As for his current mischief... It had an entirely different purpose. He cast his gaze toward Josephine as often as he could without appearing obvious about it. At last, he circled back to her, and here he meant to settle for a time. He sat across the old rug from Josephine.

"There you are, Sir Andrew." She raised that single eyebrow at him, a thing that he adored even as it drove him mad. "How do your duties as a host suit this afternoon?"

He didn't bother hiding his grin from her. "Well enough. I cannot think why you always boast of your abilities in this area, my lady. It's a simple feat to entertain pleasant company."

"Ah, that explains your ease." Her blue eyes, a perfect compliment to her gown, twinkled with amusement. "Pleasant company always provides for a delightful occasion. It is when one must also juggle the unpleasant company that hostessing becomes a challenge."

Hartwell edged into their conversation. "Sir Andrew is fortunate in his guests, especially with you as the guest of honor."

Andrew watched as Josephine lowered her gaze a moment, a slight blush creeping into her cheeks. Because of Hartwell? Usually, her blushes came and went during his spats with her. Uncertainty pricked his heart.

"I think we have a good assortment here," Andrew said, taking in the people talking and laughing, and the Hepsworth sisters conspiring. "A pleasant, informal gathering of friends. And the fine weather I ordered turned out as planned."

Josephine scoffed. "You cannot take credit for the weather."

"Are they always like this?" Hartwell said, *sotto voce,* to Simon.

"Always." Simon took another drink of his wine.

Andrew ignored them both. "Why shouldn't I take credit? I wished it fine, and here it is. A sunny morning and afternoon, just the right touch of clouds to speckle the sky, and a crisp breeze—"

"Will you claim the green of the grass was your idea, too?" Josephine wrinkled her nose at him, though that playful light remained in her eyes. This was a new sort of debate. A more pleasant one, too. In which neither of them need win. The fun was all in the argument. "Or perhaps the butterflies?"

"I ordered them painted white and green myself, yes." He gestured to the meadow. "And the birdsong was specially orchestrated to complement the meal."

"Ridiculous children." The dowager duchess tutted and rose from her chair, sending Hartwell, Simon, and Andrew scrambling to their feet. "Andrew, I am going inside your house. This spring air is all well and good for you young people, but I had rather enjoy the cool indoors. Thank you for the picnic."

"Of course, Your Grace." Andrew bowed. "May I escort you inside?"

"No. Sterling will do." She looked to the edge of the group, where the guard stood as though waiting for command. In reality, he kept watch over the scene with eyes as sharp as a falcon's. He saw the dowager duchess's gesture and came at once, offering his arm as support to lead her back to the house, where he would stay and keep watch while the other guards remained in the meadow.

Miss Hannah slipped from her place to Her Grace's vacated seat, the opportunity too good for her to resist. Andrew didn't grimace, though he and Josephine exchanged a glance. He caught Simon edging backward, too.

"Isn't this just the most delightful afternoon?" Miss Hannah asked, her voice taking on a saccharine quality that Andrew had heard her use before. On Simon. But this time, the young woman's sights were set on the baron.

Hartwell's charm extended to everyone. Even over-eager misses. "Indeed. We were just discussing the weather. Do you generally enjoy being out of doors, Miss Hannah?"

She wafted herself with her lace fan. "Oh, goodness, no. Especially as it grows warmer." She held the fan as though to cover her lips as she whispered, "I freckle terribly in the sun, you see."

"A shame." Hartwell started to turn away when she spoke again, quickly and loudly enough to discourage anyone from changing the subject.

"I understand your estate is in York, Lord Hartwell. How wonderful. I have only been to that ancient city once, but I did so admire it. Do you live in a castle, too?" Then she giggled and gestured toward Andrew's home. "Not like this one, of course. But a real castle."

Andrew bit his cheek to keep from smirking. Miss Hannah likely hadn't any idea how her comment would sound. But Josephine's eyes narrowed.

"What do you mean, a real castle?" she asked, her voice falsely sweet and yet still more soothing in sound than Miss Hannah's. "Sir Andrew's castle was built under the direction of King James, and thus predates my family's current home in age. A castle is a fortification built for the protection of the kingdom. I am quite certain Bytham Castle, new and old alike, met that criterion."

Miss Hannah blanched and flapped her fan faster. "Oh. I didn't mean—that is, Sir Andrew, you know I didn't mean anything. It's merely—well. The *size* is not what one usually thinks of when they think of castles, is it?" Her next giggle came out quite strained.

"I understood your meaning, Miss Hannah." Andrew sent a reassuring glance to Josephine, who only cocked her head to one side, her cheeks filling with color. "I took no offense. When one is used to castles such as Clairvoir, my home is not what one expects."

"I live in a large house." Hartwell had relaxed, his amusement evident. "Not a castle. And nothing so grand as Clairvoir Castle."

"Oh." The young woman's shoulders drooped. She looked at Josephine from the side of her eye. "But then, I don't suppose anywhere is as beautiful as your home, Lady Josephine."

"I have been in grander homes and palaces." Josephine smoothed her dress before tipping her chin upward. "But I find the dearest places to me have less to do with their size and a great deal more to do with the people who make them into a home. Bytham Castle—" She gestured to the structure peeking through the trees. "—has always been among my favorite places."

Andrew's heart warmed, and he had to look away to hide how her words affected him. He knew Josephine. Knew her well enough to hear the sincerity in each word she spoke. She hadn't been posturing for Miss Hannah Hepsworth, nor was she worried about defending him. She had stated a truth.

His hope, and his heart, soared.

WHEN AT LAST THE TIME CAME FOR THE PICNIC TO COME TO an end, the party made their way indoors. Josephine walked with Mrs. Hepsworth, but her gaze stayed on Andrew as he led the way through his home to the front door. The clamor had fallen to a quieter, more manageable level. The children were sun-kissed and weary; the adults yawned and spoke of napping in their carriages on the way home.

The guests staying the night excused themselves to their rooms. Even the Eastman brothers, with their two massive dogs, retired. Everyone except Josephine. Those leaving walked out the front door to their waiting carriages. Josephine went out, too, until she stood directly beside Andrew.

She stood at his side as each guest took their leave, thanking everyone for coming. The rector stood before them last, and he made a point of glancing about them before he spoke.

"I must again thank you for the invitation to attend your birthday picnic, Lady Josephine. This afternoon has been among the best I have experienced since my arrival in this county."

"You are most welcome, Mr. Wood. I am glad you enjoyed our company." Standing beside Andrew, she looked up at him with a smile on her face. Relaxed in his presence. Happy.

"And thank you, Sir Andrew, for welcoming me into your home." Mr. Wood adjusted the lapel of his coat, and a knowing gleam came into his eyes as he bowed. "Coming to know the two of you has been interesting, given our start. It seems the two of you are getting on better than when last we three met."

Josephine's cheeks warmed. She caught Andrew's startled expression from the corner of her eye. "I believe we have resigned ourselves to the fact that we enjoy each other's company." She turned her head just enough to send Andrew a slanted smile. "At least, I do not find Sir Andrew nearly as vexing as I did even a fortnight ago."

His eyes narrowed at her, and then he puffed out his chest like a preening peacock. "Vexing? You mustn't listen to her, Mr. Wood. Lady Josephine would have you believe I am the source of all contention between the two of us."

"Are you not the one who begins every argument?" she asked, arching her eyebrow at him and failing to hide her smile.

"When you use words like 'every' and 'always,' you are bound to be wrong some of the time. So I think I must firmly say no. I do not start *every* argument." He grinned with boyish delight, and that grin made her stomach drop at the same moment it caused her pulse to double in speed.

Mr. Wood chuckled and put his hands behind his back. "Do you remember the assumption I made that day you came with your questions, my lady?"

How could she forget? The rector had thought she and Andrew had arrived at his door to seek his counsel regarding marriage. Josephine darted a glance at Andrew to see his amusement replaced by curiosity. Rather than tell him the story, she slipped her hand into the crook of his arm. That was enough to make his eyes grow wide.

"I remember, Mr. Wood." She gave her attention back to the priest.

The gentleman, not much older than Andrew, broke into a wide smile. He bowed. "I hope you will remember me if things continue to change, as I suspect they will. Good day to you both." He replaced his hat, then left them to mount his borrowed horse.

Josephine waved with her free hand, as did Andrew. Then he looked down at her, his eyes narrowed. "What was all of that about?"

"I THINK I HAVE TOLD YOU BEFORE." SHE PATTED HIS ARM lightly. "What a woman says to her ecclesiastical leader is no business of anyone else." She slipped away from him, intending to re-enter the house. But Andrew caught her hand with his and tugged her gently back.

"How was your birthday picnic, Josie?" His grin had softened into something gentler, and his brown eyes were dark with sincerity. "It cannot be perfect, of course, without your parents here."

She stepped closer, their joined hands falling between them. "I had a wonderful afternoon. Thank you, Andrew, for everything. I cannot remember a birthday I enjoyed more." His gentle grip of her gloved hands momentarily tightened, then released.

"I have a gift for you."

The admission made her blink. "A gift?" No one outside her family gave her gifts, and even theirs were small tokens to show a measure of thoughtfulness. "When did you find me a gift?"

She didn't imagine his blush, or the way his gaze darted elsewhere, as though nervous. "Come inside. I want to show it to you." He held his hand out again. "Please?"

Josephine put her hand in his. She followed him, glancing up once before they entered the castle, looking at the row of windows and wondering if anyone had noticed that she was yet with Andrew.

The entryway was silent, and they slipped into the downstairs sitting room. The windows here were thrown open, and the chairs and other furnishings were warm. Arranged comfortably around the hearth, waiting for visitors to step inside and have a chat over a cup of tea.

Andrew took her through the next doorway into a room decorated in rich greens and blues, with paintings of forests and oceans all over its walls. Here a pianoforte waited along one wall, its surface well-polished and gleaming. This would be where they would sit in the evenings, she knew. A more intimate place in the castle for those invited to partake of a meal.

They went through the next set of doors. Here they came into a study with shelves along the walls, though not so many as to call the room a proper library. There were comfortable chairs drawn near the fireplace, and a desk beneath the wide window. It was here Andrew brought her, drawing her along to the desk, letting her fingers slip away from his.

A slim wooden box set in the middle of the desk. He gestured to it. "For you, Josie."

She circled the desk to sit in the leather chair behind it, and the gentle silence of the castle settled her nerves. The doors were open, and the late afternoon sunlight cast a golden glow over the room. They were alone, and all was still.

Josephine lifted the latch on the box, then opened the lid on its brass hinges. She stared at the beautiful pens inside. Three of them, their length made of wood and lightly carved to resemble ivy with the metal nibs shining on the end, bright and new. A small vial of ink rested in the velvet lining, too. The word *indigo* was scrawled on the ink's label.

She took off her gloves and laid them beside the box, then ran one finger over the center pen, admiring it. The world blurred when tears pooled in her eyes. "You remembered."

"I didn't." He stepped closer, his voice low. "I bought them the very same day we stood in front of that shop together. The moment you left, I went inside and purchased them. Even then, I think I was already half in love with you."

Josephine gasped, turning to face him, blinking. "What did you say?"

"I was halfway in love with you that day I followed you into the Burlington Arcade." His eyes glowed amber in the evening light. "I bought the pens because I knew you would love them."

"You were halfway in love?" She stepped closer to him, and this time settled her fingers on the corner of the desk. The only thing between them.

His hand came to rest beside hers, then he shook his head and gathered her hand up in both of his. His grip was gentle and warm, and so familiar. "Maybe more than half. Perhaps nearly all the way there." His smile appeared, though with less confidence than she'd ever seen him wear. "Josie. I know I have plagued you, teased and laughed at you, and I have argued with you on utterly ridiculous topics. But is there a chance, even the smallest chance, that you would grant me permission to try to win your heart?"

The tears spilled over then, even as a laugh burst from her lips. But she did not keep him waiting as she nodded, rapidly, and laid her free hand upon his cheek. "Of course you may. Yes, Andrew. If you can overlook all the times I offered you insult, or treated you without patience."

A relieved smile, then a shaky laugh, preceded Andrew putting his arm around her waist and gathering her closer. "I deserved it all, Josie. I was exasperating."

"Yes, I recall telling you as much." She tucked herself closer to him. "Andrew, you should know. I think...I think the day in the rain was the moment I thought—that I wished things were different between us." She blushed, as she had nearly every time she remembered the way he had looked at her. The two of them drenched and standing in the road. They had stood this close, then, too.

And she had thought he wanted to kiss her.

"Did you?" Mischief kindled in his eyes once more, and he bent his head. Then his gaze dropped to her lips as it had that day in the rain. "Why?"

Dare she tell him the whole of it? Admitting the truth now, with so much time wasted between them, excited as much as it frightened her. She sucked in her bottom lip and watched his eyes darken. She leaned nearer, tilting her chin upward as she whispered, "Because I'd never felt safer than when you held me in your arms."

Their lips met, the two of them coming together at the same moment and with the same gentleness. Their first kiss, tentative and curious, was far better than she'd imagined. Andrew held her against him, lips caressing hers, pulling away softly only to return immediately.

Josephine stood on her toes, and his hands steadied her as they rested upon her waist. Her hands went to his shoulders tbecause they looked strong and broad, and she wanted to feel those things for herself. They came apart with a soft gasp, and Andrew rested his forehead against hers. Josephine took in a trembling breath, then released a generous sigh.

"Josie," he murmured, his lips caressing her cheek. "Let me court you. Let me speak to your father, your brother, and secure permission to show you how I adore you, and once I have convinced you that no one is better suited for you than I am, let me marry you and bring you home to this castle. That is—" Uncertainty clouded his eyes once more. "—if you think we could be happy here, together."

His castle, where they stood at that moment, as her home? She couldn't imagine anything better. She stepped carefully away from him, smiling and blushing. They had so much to learn about this new form of communication. This new way to speak to one another, to tease one another. "Andrew." She laid her upon his chest, over his heart. "You know all my secrets but one. Wherever you are, I will be happy. Because I am already yours."

Even though she had thought it impossible to improve upon their first kiss, Andrew immediately proved her wrong.

He'd always been quite good at doing that. And this time, she would even forgive him for it.

# CHAPTER 19

S unday morning, Josephine woke when the sky was still rosy from the rising sun. The soft pinks and yellows in the sky found an answering glow in her heart. For a moment, she didn't remember what had caused such tranquil happiness, and then she remembered Andrew. Remembered those kisses stolen in the late afternoon. Her cheeks warmed, and she rolled over in her bed, clutching a pillow to her chest.

He loved her.

Considering how adamantly she protested against the idea of romance and courtship, giving in to her daydreams of both at that moment ought to embarrass her. Instead, she sighed with absolute delight and climbed from her bed. She went to the window and opened it to greet the fine spring morning.

Turning from the window, she spied the case holding her new pens on the dressing table.

How had he known, weeks and weeks ago, how perfect that gift would be for her?

Josephine went to the little trunk her maid had packed for their brief visit. She knelt beside it, opened it, and moved aside her things to pull up the false bottom. All of them had such trunks, both small and large. Hidden in each was a letter from her father, with his seal, to anyone willing to give his children safe passage or sanctuary. A banknote with a large sum, and small purse with coins, also made up the emergency cache. What had happened to the French nobility during their bloody revolution hadn't ever dimmed in the duke's mind.

"If it can happen in France, it can happen anywhere," he would tell his children. "It gives me peace of mind, these small things we do."

Josephine smiled fondly as she moved those things aside. Small things. Having guards follow them around nearly everywhere didn't feel *small*. But for a man as powerful as the duke, she supposed it made sense.

Beneath her father's added measure of security lay the thing she searched for. A large packet of paper. She had brought it on a whim, telling herself she needn't follow through with her idea if something changed.

Josephine needed help. She needed someone else to look at what she had written. Andrew was the perfect someone, with Emma still in London busy with learning what it meant to be wife to an ambassador.

She took one of those beautiful pens and dipped it in the deep blue ink, then scrawled a note directly on the brown paper.

*To Andrew: You needn't read it unless you wish, but if you do, I look forward to discussing it with someone I admire and trust.*

She ended the scrawl with an elegant letter J.

Without the aid of her maid, Josephine dressed simply. She would prepare for morning services after her errand. It shouldn't take long.

Sneaking about someone else's castle wasn't exactly as easy as sneaking about her own. Especially carrying a manuscript wrapped up in brown paper and tied with string. She had written Andrew's name on it and intended to leave it on the desk where he had given her the beautiful pens.

The rejected manuscript. The story that she had read and re-read and couldn't understand why that publisher wanted nothing to do with it. Maybe Andrew would understand. He was the only one, other than her dearest Emma, Josephine trusted to read and give an honest opinion without hurting her.

Their talk the day before, the way he had looked at Josephine as though he'd reordered his world with her at its center, gave her every confidence that he would be kind. Their history up to the point reassured her he would tell the truth.

She paused atop the staircase when she heard men's voices from farther down the corridor. Though she couldn't make out the words, she knew Roman and Lyness were the speakers. Nibbling on her lip, Josephine moved with greater speed and less stealth all the way down the stairs.

It was easy enough to get to the study. The servants were all busy with breakfast preparations at this early hour. Once she had safely deposited the packet on the desk, Josephine retraced her steps through the quiet ground floor.

When she eased out of the sitting room, she turned to close the doors carefully behind her. And then—

"Lady Josephine."

She stilled and turned around, her heart racing with surprise. And guilt. Because Lord Hartwell had spoken her name from midway down the stairs. He wore riding boots and appeared dressed to go out. She swallowed.

"Good morning, Lord Hartwell." She curtsied, aware that her hair was inelegantly piled atop her head, of course, but mortified by the knowledge she had misled this man. However uninten-tionally.

He came another step down, slowly. "You are up early. Here I thought I was the only one who rose with the sun." He appeared friendly enough, but she sensed something stirring beneath his cheerful expression. Something sad.

"This is not the usual thing for me, I assure you." She tried to smile, but it felt weak upon her face.

"I wonder if you would step outside with me for a moment?" he asked, gesturing to the front door. "I will not take much of your time. I know it is too early. If you would like to fetch a maid—?"

Josephine shook her head. "That won't be necessary. Sterling informed my brother there would be a guard at the door."

His eyebrows went up. "Truly?"

"My father takes our safety quite seriously." She pulled her shawl tighter and came to the foot of the steps. Waiting for him. Knowing, somehow, what it was he wished to say. She owed him a conversation, at the very least. Lord Hartwell, a good and honorable man, deserved her honesty.

He opened the door and allowed her to step out first. Birdsong filled the trees around the little castle, and the whispers of a breeze twined through the branches and leaves. And there, standing before the house in plain brown clothing, was Sterling himself.

Sterling was her favorite of the guards. He'd never treated her with anything other than respect, and she had the sense that his honor was as strong as any nobleman's. Her father called the guard a man of integrity, and her father's opinion counted more than most.

The guard bowed upon seeing her and the baron, then he spoke in a somewhat rough voice. "My lady, may I be of assistance?"

They had coded phrases she could use to signal distress, but this morning she relaxed. "Lord Hartwell and I are going to wander that way and have a conversation." She pointed to the nearest tree. "If you will act as chaperone for a moment, that is all I require."

He bowed again, then stood straight and still as a statue.

Hartwell tucked his hands behind his back and walked with her to the tree, looking over his shoulder only once. "I never imagined things might be difficult enough that your father would hire his own guard."

"As of yet, I have not experienced a great need for them. But I am grateful my father cares enough to have them, just the same." Josephine folded her arms tightly against her chest and stopped, her shoes growing damp in the grass. "You had something you wished to say, Lord Hartwell."

He stood an arm's length away, and in the dappled shadows of the tree, she saw the regret in his eyes. "I do have something to say. I hope you will not think me uncouth for saying it, either. First, I wish to tell you that I am not offended, nor do I mean any offense by this conversation. I have the greatest respect for you, my lady, and your family."

She nodded her understanding, her throat growing tight.

"From the first, since I saw you and Sir Andrew together at the castle, I sensed a connection between the two of you. When first your brother, then you, assured me it was nothing but friend-ship, I ignored my instincts. But I have eyes, my lady. When I saw the two of you together yesterday, especially as you tended to your guests together, I knew at once there is more there. You cannot hide that kind of affection, I think."

Josephine felt her cheeks warm, and she lowered her gaze to the grass between them. "I am terribly sorry, my lord. I swear to you, when you asked if my affections were settled elsewhere, I didn't know at the time what I have since recognized as truth. I did not mean to deceive you." It was the most she could say and maintain the bounds of propriety. An unwed lady didn't go about discussing her hopes or her affections for a man until things had been settled between families. Even if her feelings were quite obvious.

"I did not think the deception intentional." He chuckled, and she looked up with hope. Giving insult was the last thing she wished to do. And his accepting smile eased her conscience. "You are a fine lady, Josephine Dinard. Sir Andrew is a fortunate man to have your affection."

"Thank you." Her estimation of him went upward. "I am certain there is a lady better for you than I am, Lord Hartwell."

His eyes turned sad again. "We will see. But in the meantime, I think it best that I take my leave this morning, before Sunday services. My brother and I will return to your family's castle to gather the rest of our things, then we will go on to York." He cleared his throat. "I will make up an excuse. You needn't worry that I will say anything in regard to our situation, my lady. As always, you have my respect."

Despite his words, his kindness, the man had suffered a hurt. She didn't know him well enough to know if it was more than pride, though it had to be less than heartbreak given the brevity of their relationship. But she did not mind his desire to save face.

"I wish you a safe journey, my lord."

He bowed, and then walked away. Leaving her to stand beneath the trees alone while he passed Sterling and entered the house. She took a deep breath and closed her eyes. When she opened them, the guard approached, his eyes sweeping this way and that, much like a shepherd dog when keeping watch over sheep.

"My lady." He bowed again. "Are you well?"

"Yes, Sterling. Thank you. For everything." She smiled and he kept to her side as she made her way back to the front door.

Not an hour later, a knock at her bedroom door made Josephine look up from the mirror. Her maid, Susan, was putting the finishing touches on Josephine's hair. She wore a simple dress, with delicate lace at the sleeves and throat, appropriate for a morning spent in church.

"Who is it?" she called, meeting Susan's eyes in the mirror.

"One most unaccustomed to knocking on doors," came the rumbly answer. The dowager duchess had risen earlier than usual.

Susan didn't need to be told to rush to the door to open it, while Josephine came to her feet. Susan curtsied once the door was fully open, and when Her Grace strode in, Susan slipped out and closed the door behind her.

"Grandmama. Good morning." Josephine curtsied as she spoke, then approached her grandmother to give her a kiss on the cheek.

"My dear girl." Her Grace took Josephine gently by the shoulders and looked deeply into her eyes, as though she could see into her granddaughter's thoughts. "Lord Hartwell and his brother have just left. On urgent business, the baron said. He also said he had already taken his leave of you. My dear, you do not have an understanding with him?"

Josephine shook her head. "No, Grandmama. We are—and will remain—friends only."

Her grandmother relaxed. "Good. I hoped as much, especially watching you with Andrew yesterday." She made her way to the chair Josephine had just vacated and settled there with all the dignity of a queen sitting upon a throne. "I assume that is why the baron left with such expediency?"

Josephine blushed. "Yes, Grandmama. It seems yesterday was a revelation for several of us." She worried the bracelet at her wrist, a gift from her father on her birthday the year previous. "I am sorry if I acted in any way inappropriately—"

"Not at all, my dear. No, there is nothing to worry about on that account." Her grandmother sighed, and then her eyes took on a gentle light. "Look at you. All grown up and in love."

"You do not seem surprised."

"Child, I have known that you and our baronet were meant for one another for some time." The slow upward curl of her lips, the arch of a single brow, made her grandmother look quite smug. And finally, Josephine laughed.

"You tried to hint as much to me—oh my goodness. When you told me you thought Andrew jealous, you meant he was jealous of

Lord Hartwell." Josephine couldn't help the laugh that escaped as she sat upon the edge of her bed. "Grandmama, why didn't you say something? Something besides your hinting."

"You wouldn't have listened." Grandmama sniffed daintily and fiddled with the pen on Josephine's desk. "You are too much like me. You have to discover things for yourself before you believe them."

"Then you approve?" Josephine asked, heart rising with hope. If her grandmother approved, so too would her parents. They loved Andrew, of course, but that didn't mean they would immediately think a baronet worthy of their daughter's hand in marriage. If, she told herself, it went so far. If Andrew didn't change his mind. If he really, truly loved her.

The dowager duchess smiled warmly at her granddaughter, then answered with great amusement, "Of course I approve, my darling. You two are a perfect fit for one another. I think you will make each other happy, and what's more, I think he's more than clever enough for you to match wits with throughout your life."

Josephine rose and went to wrap her arms around her grandmother, relieved and hopeful beyond words.

WHO WOULD HAVE GUESSED THAT SHARING A HYMNAL WITH a woman could lead to such a feeling of connection? Andrew had certainly never considered what the simple act of holding a book by one end while Josephine held the other would do to his heart. It flipped. It danced. It hummed happily along with the music. All things, he well knew, a heart ought not to do.

When Hartwell had taken his leave, full of apologetic words and meaningful glances, Andrew hadn't known what Josephine would say. How it might make her feel. But she seemed happier than ever, sitting beside him in the old medieval church, her shoulder brushing his as they listened to the vicar's sermon and raised their own voices in song.

But everything had changed. From the moment he woke that morning, the world had taken on a brighter cast. The air was sweeter, the sky brighter, and his body stronger than it had ever been before. All because he knew Josephine returned his feelings. He felt it, within his very soul, and life could only grow the better for having told her of his affection for her.

At the end of the service, Andrew followed Simon and the dowager duchess out of the chapel. The governess kept behind with the younger girls. Once they were out of doors, Andrew looked down into Josephine's eyes and murmured, "Someday soon, I hope to introduce you to everyone here."

She colored, as though she knew he had wished to add the words "as my wife" to his claim. But they still had weeks and weeks before he could imagine having the banns read. He needed to give her a proper courtship. Before they could court in earnest, he must make the journey back to London to ask her father's permission.

And before all that, he must tell Simon. And hope his friend did not see this change as a betrayal of trust. They had always told each other everything. They were as near to one another as brothers, lacking only the blood to make them so.

After Andrew helped Josephine and her sisters step into the carriage, Simon caught his shoulder, and the duke's son spoke in low tones directly into Andrew's ear. "You and I need to talk."

Andrew nodded his understanding, and then the two of them went to the gig that Andrew kept at his estate. The two of them followed the carriage as it left the churchyard.

Simon didn't wait long to break the silence. "I have never seen a man look as relieved as you did when you bid Hartwell and his brother goodbye this morning."

Andrew tipped his hat farther back, then held the reins in

both hands. "It wasn't that they left that caused such a thing. It was what Hartwell said, about Josephine, before he went."

"That struck me as curious." Simon folded his arms and slouched in his seat, casting Andrew a suspicious look. "He had already taken leave of Josephine. But he didn't seem inclined to comment anything more. I thought he meant to court her, but that no longer appears to be his intention."

"No." Andrew relaxed his grip on the reins. "And I am sorry for him. He is a good fellow." His gut twisted. How did he say what he wished to say, without sounding like a fool?

"Among the best." Andrew shifted nervously on his seat. Then cleared his throat. "There's something I need to tell you."

Simon raised one lordly eyebrow. "Oh?" He wasn't going to make it any easier for Andrew than that.

"I told Josephine that I am in love with her."

Simon sat all the way up. "You what?" he asked, the words a bark of surprise.

Andrew's heart sank. "I told your sister I love her. Yesterday. But I have felt it coming on for some time—"

"'Coming on?' You make it sound like a head cold." Simon chuckled, and the sound startled Andrew enough that he gaped at his friend, pulling back on the reins enough to make the horse slow its steps. "I hope that isn't the wording you used when you informed her of your feelings."

"Not—not quite." Andrew turned forward, then faced his friend again. "I thought you would be shocked."

"I am. That is, I'm surprised. But it also makes sense." Simon shook his head and sighed. "Why couldn't you have figured this out before I invited Hartwell to visit?"

"I wasn't ready to admit it yet." Andrew ducked his head somewhat sheepishly. "Hartwell's visit acted as something of an accelerator. Of sorts."

Simon snorted. "I suppose you're welcome for that."

Andrew chuckled, the worry within him untangling itself. "You don't mind then?"

"About you and Josephine? Not at all." Simon's grin turned lazy. "This will make you my brother in truth, which pleases me to no end. Do you think you will stop bickering with Josephine, or will love accelerate *that,* too?"

"I think we'll always bicker." He looked to the carriage ahead, thinking of the woman he loved riding inside. "But all our arguments will come to far sweeter conclusions."

Simon groaned. "Oh, no. You're going to be one of those sorts— the poetical suitor. Do save it for Josephine, won't you? Spare the rest of us your lovemaking as much as possible." Simon leaned back again. "And treat her well, Andrew. She deserves the best you can give her."

"On that, we are in agreement." Andrew was ready to change the subject, if only to grant his friend the mercy of not discussing his sister and romance at the same time.

But Simon spoke before Andrew could, changing the subject himself. "I haven't told anyone, but Father and Mother mean to return to the castle tomorrow, as a surprise visit, before Father returns to London for the rest of the parliamentary session."

"That's marvelous news." Andrew guided the horse into the lane that would take them to his home. "Everyone will be delighted."

"I know you meant to stay in Bytham longer, to see to your affairs. But I think you should come back with us." Simon's eyes narrowed, calculating. "It will be the perfect opportunity to speak to my father about courting Josephine."

The relief Andrew had felt after confessing to Simon vanished. Speaking to the duke on the morrow meant a return to anxiety. He gulped, then nodded. "I agree. I will arrange to return with you this afternoon."

Simon's laugh was almost wicked. "An excellent decision, baronet."

Hours later, Andrew followed the duke's carriage. He'd told a curious Josephine that he felt it best to return to Clairvoir with them, for safety's sake. He wouldn't spoil her parents' surprise for anything. But, unsettled as he was to think of speaking of her father, he couldn't deny to himself what a relief it was to be with her longer.

In his trunk was her manuscript, which he'd found that morning on his desk. And he couldn't wait to read it. Hopefully, as he kept her company in her tower, away from prying eyes, where he might well sneak a kiss or two. But mostly he would sit quietly, supporting the woman he loved as she wrote, encouraging each and every one of her dreams.

# EPILOGUE

*June 1819*

The ballroom of the castle wasn't hidden behind closed doors, but rather stood as an open hall at the top of a wide staircase. When the family hosted parties, the music drifted through the corridors of the castle. Here, Josephine and Andrew would greet their guests after they were married in the family chapel.

Emma, Josephine's dearest friend, sat at a table in the center of the hall. As did the duchess and the dowager duchess. Spread before them were lists of guests, small flower arrangements, and ribbons in every color imaginable.

"I still cannot believe you are marrying Andrew." Emma checked another name off the list before shooting Josephine a conspiratorial grin. "You two have detested one another for ages."

Josephine blushed and looked across the room to where Andrew leaned against the stair rail, speaking to Simon. "I never exactly disliked him, you know."

"Oh, we know." Her mother turned over another lace sample for the bridal veil. "The spirited arguments over the years were nothing more than you two falling deeply in love with one another." She laughed when Josephine narrowed her eyes. "My darling, I am grateful this day has come. But after the misery the two of you put us through, always making us listen to your debates, every member of this family is entitled to a little teasing."

"Hear, hear," Grandmama added beneath her breath. She unceremoniously picked up a purple ribbon and tossed it into a basket of rejected fabrics and flowers. "We really ought to use the blue for your hair and the flowers," she said, picking up two blue ribbons.

Josephine didn't much care what she wore. She'd be happy in an old flour sack, so long as she married Andrew in two weeks' time. "The blue would be lovely. Thank you, Grandmama."

"And Irish lace, I think." Her Grace, the Duchess of Montfort, picked up a beautiful piece that mimicked vines and flowers. "To honor our family's ties to Ireland. Unless you would prefer the French." She picked up a daintier piece.

"The Irish lace," Josephine said, looking over her shoulder again at Andrew only to find him grinning back at her as Simon spoke. Her betrothed had wanted to offer her a longer courtship, but with the uncertainty of her father's political schedule, Josephine had thrown all caution to the wind. "Why don't you marry me now?" she had asked the day after her father had given his approval of the match.

Andrew, after an initial moment of surprise, had pulled her close and kissed her where they stood, in the middle of her tower room. Then he'd held her hand while reading her manuscript, and she pretended to read a book of poetry. His thumb, brushing her knuckles gently, had proven quite distracting.

"You see?" Emma's voice said, interrupting Josephine's memory. "It is no use talking to her when my cousin is within sight. We ought to dismiss them both."

"I quite agree." The duchess's soft smile was one of approval rather than impatience. "You have made enough decisions for now, my dear. Why don't you and Andrew take a walk in the gardens? I am certain you have much to discuss."

They did—and they would have the rest of their lives to speak of anything and everything. But Josephine rose from the table with enthusiasm, kissing first her mother and then her grandmother, before walking across the room to her beloved.

Andrew held his hand out as she approached, and she took it in her own before snuggling into his side. "I have been told that you and I must go on a walk," she told him, then gave her brother an apologetic smile. "If you don't mind me kidnapping my betrothed."

"Not in the least. He's been standing here mooning over you the whole time." Simon pushed away from the rail, a wide smile on his face. "Maybe a little air and exercise will make you both fit for company again." He winked at them, then sauntered toward the stairs.

Andrew took her in the opposite direction, through a corridor and down the steps that would take them out into the air in the fewest amount of steps. Together, they stepped into the bright afternoon sunlight. He tucked her close as they walked.

"Wedding preparations going well?" he asked, his eyes dancing with happiness.

"Exceedingly so, though I am sick of them. I wish you would have let Father procure us a special license. We could've been married yesterday, or the day before."

"Your mother and grandmother would be distressed," he reminded her. "You're the first daughter, the first granddaughter, to wed. It will be a wonderful occasion, and then I will spirit you away for our wedding trip." He slowed their walk when they neared a stone bench, and there he brought her.

"I cannot wait for our adventure." She sat beside him and raised her chin to accept the kiss she knew he would give her. His lips touched hers, full of certainty and love. She returned the token of affection with her whole heart, sliding her hand from his shoulder to cradle the back of his head.

When Andrew held her in his arms, she knew the two of them could do anything together. That they belonged to one another. That somehow, despite all their arguments and teasing over the years, they were meant to share their lives and their hearts with one another.

"I love you, Josie," he murmured against her lips when they paused for breath.

She tipped her forehead to rest against his. "I love you, too."

"What? You aren't going to make me call you Lady Josephine anymore?"

"Only when I am very cross with you." She kissed him, a quick touch of her lips to his. "Otherwise, I am happy to be your Josie for the rest of my life."

Forever and always in love, Josie and Andrew would build a beautiful life together. Of that, she had no doubt. Because what better way for her to continue their story than within the words "they lived happily ever after?"

Simon leaned against the cannon they had placed at the end of the Guard Room, listening as his sister and his best friend laughed together, walking down the corridor. They were happier than he'd ever seen them, as unlikely a match as he thought them.

Andrew had told him once that he didn't know when he would've taken a chance with Josephine if Simon hadn't invited Hartwell to visit. But Simon never would've invited another onto the field of courtship if he'd guessed at his friend's feelings.

Down the long entry hall, the door to the duke's small study— the Speak a Word room, the family called it—opened. One day, it would be Simon who sat inside that room, at the desk, making time for tenants, servants, and neighbors alike who "needed only to speak a word" with the duke.

Someday far in the future, he hoped.

The duke stepped into view, and Simon straightened. When his father caught sight of him, the duke made a motion for Simon to join him.

Crossing the expanse between them, Simon's shoes clicking against the black-and-white marble floor, didn't take long. The duke motioned for his son to enter the study, then closed the door behind them both.

"I need a word with you, Simon."

A cold chill went down Simon's spine, though he tried to sound amused as he countered, "I thought that's what people said to you in this room."

His father quirked an eyebrow at him. "Usually." He gestured to the chair across from the desk. When he took his usual seat on the other side, Simon realized whatever the subject under discussion was, it was serious.

Sometimes, when they sat across a table or stood across the room from one another, Simon fancied that he looked into a mirror that showed what and who he would be in the future. His father had passed most of his physical traits onto his son. Simon could only hope his father had passed on the qualities that had made him a duke beloved by the people under his care and respected by his peers throughout Europe.

"How did you enjoy your time in Ireland?" the duke asked, the question weighted as more than a curious inquiry.

Ireland? He'd returned from their Irish estate nearly a year before. The Farleigh earldom had been a gift from the king to their family generations before. "I thought my time there well spent. The tenants are good people. The land is lush and beautiful. I would gladly return if there's a need."

An approving smile appeared on his father's face, but he shook his head to that offer. "There isn't a need. Yet. But the Irish

227

voices in Parliament grow louder and more concerned, especially for the Catholics both in Ireland and throughout the kingdom. I have given a lot of thought to the matter, and I believe we should do more on their behalf with our influence."

The ducal influence was what his father meant, of course. But it stirred Simon just the same, to know his father shared his decisions, political and otherwise, with his son.

"Teague Frost, Lord Dunmore, caught my attention in Parliament. He's around your age. Maybe a few years older. He'll return to Ireland before next Season, of course, but I thought to invite him to stay with us in December."

"For the Christmas celebrations?" Simon chuckled. "You know Mother doesn't like us politicking during the holidays."

"We won't be. Much." The duke's eyes twinkled. "I spoke to her about it, of course. She said if we intended to make a house party of it, she had to have a say in the guests, too. Of course, Lord Dunmore will bring his family with him."

"Is he a married man?" Simon hadn't met many lordlings his age willing to settle, unless they'd already inherited their estates and titles. It was awkward to take a wife while on an allowance, as many of his friends were. But seeing Andrew and Josephine's happiness, even Emma's and her count's, had started to make him wonder if, perhaps, he needed to reconsider his own opinions on marriage.

His father shook his head. "He has a mother, younger brother, and sister. The brother is a Catholic priest."

Simon couldn't help raising his eyebrows at that. "But Lord Dunmore claims Anglicanism?"

The duke gave a knowing nod. "As he must, to be allowed to sit in Lords."

"Interesting." Simon folded his arms and sat back in his chair. "Lady Dunmore and Miss Frost would accompany Dunmore for Christmas?"

"I should hope so."

"That is still many months away."

The duke put his elbows on his desk and clasped his hands beneath his chin. "But Dunmore is in London now, without the ladies. After Josephine's wedding, if you return with me, I can introduce the two of you. I'd like your opinion of him before I extend the invitation."

A swell of pride threatened to puff Simon up that very moment, but he swallowed it back and sat straight in his chair. "Of course, Father. I have no doubt I will agree with your assessment. I'm certain December will see us greeting Lord Dunmore and his ladies here at the castle."

He couldn't help the grin he wore as he left the room a short time later. An Irishman and his family for Christmas.

One thing was for certain. Life at the castle was never dull.

ARE YOU CURIOUS ABOUT SIMON'S UPCOMING STORY, *LORD Farleigh and Miss Frost*? Order it now on Amazon.com and get ready for a magical Christmas at Clairvoir Castle.

And don't forget to sign up for Sally's newsletter to stay informed about ALL her upcoming books, series, and **TOP SECRET** updates.

# AUTHOR'S NOTES

Important Historical Note: The unrest in England that I mentioned throughout the book was quite real. In the year 1819, there were many protests, large crowds of British citizens listening to political leaders, and all of this culminated in an event now called the Peterloo Massacre on August 16, 1819. British citizens were attacked, charged by the 15th Hussars with their sabers drawn. It's estimated that fifteen people were killed and between 400-600 people injured.

A peaceful rally was attacked by armed calvary. It was a tragedy. Sadly, it still took time for the British laws to change in a way which favored the working classes. It's an interesting part of history that I highly recommend my readers explore.

On a happier note, I introduced several new characters in this story, and I know you might be curious about them.

John Sterling, the handsome young guard.

Jonathan Wood, the rector with an interest in the Clairvoir chapel.

Roman and Lyness Eastwood, the brothers from York.

All four of these gentlemen have stories to tell. Sterling and

Wood will have tales that are part of the Clairvoir Castle series. I'm truly excited to share them in the future.

Roman and Lyness will be part of a brand new series coming in 2023.

To keep up with all my news and announcements of new books and series, join my newsletter! You can do that by visiting my website, www.AuthorSallyBritton.com.

The Clairvoir Castle series has been a wonderful project for me. Those who have read books I've written outside of it will notice a difference in tone. My other books tend to contain more serious topics and situations, and they're also (usually) longer. The Clairvoir Castle series was originally written in response to the early days of the COVID-19 Pandemic, when people were scared, stressed, and tired of "doom scrolling." I wanted to write something easier on the mind and heart for myself and for my readers. I hope this series continues to be an escape, lighter love stories, for all my readers.

I want to thank my incredible editor, Jenny Proctor of Midnight Owl Editing, for helping me set this story straight. Jenny is a dream to work with and so uplifting.

Many thanks also to my best friend, Shaela Kay, for letting me rant, cry, laugh, and bounce ideas off of her. Everyone should have a Shaela.

Special thanks also to my incredible assistant, Marilee Merrell, who runs so much behind the scenes! This book would've taken much longer to write without her help.

And to my Squad - THANK YOU. This book is dedicated to you wonderful ladies for many reasons.

Last but most importantly, thank you to my husband, my children, my family. Their love and support mean the world to me. I am grateful for each moment I have with them.

## ALSO BY SALLY BRITTON

**Castle Clairvoir Romances:**

*Mr. Gardiner and the Governess* | *A Companion for the Count*

*Sir Andrew and the Authoress* | *Lord Farleigh and Miss Frost*

**The Inglewood Series:**

*Rescuing Lord Inglewood* | *Discovering Grace*

*Saving Miss Everly* | *Engaging Sir Isaac*

*Reforming Lord Neil*

**The Branches of Love Series:**

*Martha's Patience* | *The Social Tutor*

*The Gentleman Physician* | *His Bluestocking Bride*

*The Earl and His Lady* | *Miss Devon's Choice*

*Courting the Vicar's Daughter* | *Penny's Yuletide Wish*

**Stand Alone Regency Romances:**

*The Captain and Miss Winter* | *His Unexpected Heiress*

*A Haunting at Havenwood* | *Her Unsuitable Match*

*An Unsuitable Suitor* | *A Mistletoe Mismatch*

**Hearts of Arizona Series:**

*Silver Dollar Duke* | *Copper for the Countess* | *A Lady's Heart of Gold*

# ABOUT THE AUTHOR

Sally Britton, along with her husband, their four incredible children, their tabby Willow, and their dogs Izzie and Frosty, live in Oklahoma. So far, they really like it there, even if the family will always consider Texas home.

Sally started writing her first story on her mother's electric typewriter when she was fourteen years old. Reading her way through Jane Austen, Louisa May Alcott, and Lucy Maud Montgomery, Sally decided to write about the complex world of centuries past.

Sally graduated from Brigham Young University in 2007 with a bachelor's in English. She met and married her husband not long after and started working on their happily ever after.

Vincent Van Gogh is attributed with the quote, "What is done in love is done well." Sally has taken that as her motto, writing stories where love is a choice.

All of Sally's published works are available on Amazon.com and you can connect with Sally and sign up for her newsletter on her website, AuthorSallyBritton.com.

Made in United States
North Haven, CT
30 June 2024